Cover Design and Interior Format

WHISPERS FROM THE PAST

AUSTRALIAN BESTSELLING AUTHOR

KAYE DOBBIE

PROLOGUE

❧

1908

S UNLIGHT BEAMED THROUGH THE ENOR-
MOUS stained glass window at the end of the
empty corridor. A sheet of blue, speckled with
intricate glass birds: blackbirds, thrushes, sparrows,
robins. English birds. They hung forever silent in
their blue glass sky.

It was Sunday and the great house was nearly
empty. Only two voices rose and fell in the tail-end
of a bitter quarrel. Porcelain smashed and some
piece of furniture was overturned. There was the
sound of a hard hand against soft flesh. A muffled
scream. The timbre of the argument changed as the
air was charged with violence.

A woman burst from one of the rooms, the door
banging loudly behind her. Her silver brocade
slippers skimmed the floor but her evening dress,
with its long skirt and short train, prevented her
from gaining any real pace. A heavy ruby circled
by pearls hung low on her breast, rising and falling
with each swift breath. Hair the colour of butter
was held back by sparkling slides with two loose
curls at her temples. Her small, pointed face would
have been pretty in repose, but when she reached

the top of the staircase and looked back, all beauty had been erased by stark white terror.

The soft click of a door opening echoed in the corridor behind her. The woman snatched her skirts up almost to her knees, disclosing slim silk-stockinged legs, and began to descend the stairs. A man had come out of the room and stood dark and faceless against the big blue window. The woman missed a step and stumbled, only just regaining her balance as she reached the entrance hall.

It stretched before her, shadowy doorways at intervals down its length in an elegant clutter of lush potted ferns, ornate pedestals, smooth marble statues and gilt-framed paintings. The floor was tiled in precise black and white squares, beckoning her forward to the grand front door. Beyond that door lay the circular drive and the garden. There was just a slight chance that someone might be out there – the gardener or one of his minions. Just a chance that someone might see or hear her and come to her rescue.

Her only chance.

Behind her she heard the soft, sinister creak of the treads. He was following. She took off at a run down the chequered hall, just as a large white cat ran across the tiles in front of her, its claws scrabbling at the smooth surface as it struggled to gain purchase. With a startled cry, she turned sharply into one of the doorways, and her only chance was gone.

Panicking now, she darted through an arch into the music room. Heavy velvet curtains were drawn over the bay windows and the pressed metal ceiling soared above her. The piano and the harp became menacing shapes in the gloom. The air was sickly sweet with the heavy scent from a bowl of late roses: *Mme Isaac Pereire,* large and full and exquisite. She slowed, the jumbled memories like storm clouds in her mind, thinking how she had picked and arranged those roses herself, just yesterday.

How could that be? How could this be happening . . .

His outline filled the doorway; death in a three-piece suit.

She had meant to get back into the entrance hall through the dining room, but seeing him there, all sense of direction deserted her. She cannoned into the harp, sending it to the parquet floor with a loud crash. Now the library door was before her and she flung herself through: books, leather-bound with tooled gold lettering, pages musty with tobacco smoke. And beyond the library was a narrow corridor. The smell of last night's roast beef drifted up the steep kitchen stairs. Last night they had had guests and there had been noise and laughter. Now the silence was as heavy as her heartbeat.

Above her on the second floor a clock began to strike. Oddly, the sound calmed her. Three o'clock. It was three o'clock. Another hour and the servants would begin to return.

If only she could stay alive for one more hour . . .

The kitchen stairs were so steep, the evening dress made negotiating them difficult. Light-headed she wondered why she had let him persuade her to put the dress on. 'Exquisite,' he had said, with that smile of his. 'Superb.' And like a silly girl she had believed him.

The kitchen was empty, the remains of a cold

luncheon still scattered about. Behind her a soft step warned of his approach. The door to the back garden was locked and the key gone. Far too many moments were wasted as she struggled with it. She spun about, ready to fight, and caught sight of that other door across the room – the door to the tunnel.

And it was open.

Eagerly, she blundered around the scrubbed table. The tunnel had not been used for ages. Not since summer last year when some visitors had asked for a tour. It was dangerous, and even as she ran through into the dark a warning voice was asking why it was open now.

A lantern hanging from a cobwebbed beam flared in the sudden draft. A lighted lantern in this abandoned place? How could that be . . . Bewildered she ran on and saw another and then another showing her the way. His plan was monstrous and cruel: he had meant her to come this way all along. He had been directing her, subtly and heartlessly, into his trap.

She cried out, but there was no way back now. She took another step, and then another. The thin sole of her slipper found a damp place and she slipped and fell, just saving herself as she reached out, but grazing the skin on her knuckles. The earthy, mouldy smell caught in her throat and made her want to cough.

Or scream.

But who would she scream for? There was no one apart from him, and he had no pity. She should have realised that long ago. Maybe she had: maybe that had been part of the thrill of having him. The little cruelties, the savagery of his smile . . . To have such a man in her power – or so she had thought. And all the while he had just been playing at love.

A sob rose in her chest. Ahead of her the tunnel made a turn. As she scrambled around it she suddenly saw the steep descent. The smell of the sea was all about her. It would be grey on a day like this, sullen, the sky and the water as one. But the sea didn't frighten her; it never had. She pushed off from the wall – bare rock now – feeling a new surge of strength. Her hair was coming down over her shoulders, her dress was dirty and torn, her skin bruised and bleeding, but suddenly she had hope.

If she could reach the opening at the bottom . . . If it was clear of rock and sand . . . If she didn't fall again . . . If the tide was in . . .

She was good at swimming. She could swim like a fish, naked in the cold sea, his arms around her, salt on his lips.

My love, my love, my only love . . .

Behind her came the scuff of his shoes on some loose stones as he continued his relentless pursuit. Knowing she should not, she glanced back, thinking even at this stage that it had to be a mistake, some foolish joke gone wrong. But she saw his face, just once and that was enough.

'Help me!' she gasped. *'Au secours!'*

The Frenchwoman ran.

CHAPTER I

1928

THE DOORBELL CHIMED SOFTLY INSIDE the house, competing with a popular jazz quartet on the wireless. Daniel met Evie's nervous glance with a wink. He looked the part in his grey suit. It was their biggest case yet, although he didn't appear to be any less confident than usual. But then that was Daniel's talent, pretending to be something he wasn't.

Evie turned back to the garden, to the wavering lanterns and moths. Here on the south side of the Yarra the very wealthy lived in isolation. The Jones's estate seemed a long way from Evie's house in Earle Street, but in reality it was barely two miles. Although reality, Evie found, had little to do with the very rich.

It was a warm summer evening with only a slight breeze – enough to stir the hem of her new dress. Black with thin shoulder straps, it dipped at the back and exposed far more skin than Evie was used to. Her shoes were new, too, the latest thing, with cut-outs over the instep. Daniel had bought the outfit for her so she could look the part.

'You're in disguise, Evie,' he told her. 'A beautiful, mysterious woman. Untouchable, unreachable. Closer to the spirit world than this one.'

He had bought the veil, too. The sheer black net attached to her fair hair turned her face into a blur. 'Perfect,' he'd said when he picked her up in the car this evening. His fingertips flicked her cheek warmly. His eyes shone with a creator's pride.

The door opened and the music was suddenly louder. 'Mr Roxburgh! At last!'

Muriel Nelson, widow of the late Howard Jones, *Melbourne Clarion* tycoon, and lately remarried, came forward smiling. The beaded fringes of her pale pink dress swung jauntily. She had a cigarette in a long holder and her auburn hair was cropped as short as a boy's. Though not in the flush of youth, she was striking, with a lean figure perfectly suited to the fashions. Her face was heavily made-up in Clara Bow style, with kohl-rimmed eyes and blood-red lips.

'We'd begun to think you weren't coming,' she said with a pout.

Daniel smiled. He had an attractive smile which couldn't help but impress. Evie had noticed that most of his clients were women. They were probably all in love with him.

'The motor car needed a few repairs.' He was explaining away their lateness in a suave English accent. 'I'm most terribly sorry, Mrs Nelson.'

He didn't sound sorry, but Muriel Nelson didn't seem to care. Her eyes skimmed past him to the driveway and noted the gleaming Oldsmobile.

'Call me Muriel,' she said, and twisted a finger in the double string of beads about her throat.

'Muriel.' That smile again. 'This is Miss Evangeline Woodward.' Daniel drew Evie forward. He always used her full name because he said it made her sound like a film star.

'Miss Woodward.' Muriel took in the veil. If Muriel Nelson was Clara Bow, then Evie was Greta Garbo.

She led them down a long hallway. There was a spotlit painting on the wall with its jangling colours applied thickly and, to the uninitiated, amateurishly. Boxes and rectangles stacked in an untidy pile. Evie was sure it was worth thousands.

'I have some people waiting. I hope you don't mind? I couldn't keep something like this to myself.'

She took them into a large room at the back of the house where a cocktail party was in progress. About half a dozen bored people looked up at Evie and Daniel. Fashionable clothing, glittering jewellery and faces flushed from alcohol and the Black Bottom. Evie could see their eyes literally light up at the prospect of Something New.

The décor was subdued, with ecru walls and a huge silver framed mirror over the fireplace. A big red and brown African rug lay on the polished floor surrounded by chairs and a sofa. Glasses, coffee cups and an ivory inlaid cigarette box cluttered a low table. The jazz quartet Evie had heard from the door bubbled out of the wireless.

The introductions were made. Friendly but businesslike, Daniel shook hands, while Evie smiled mysteriously and stood back. Daniel was impressive, she had to give him that. Tall, dark and well-dressed, he was very much the part he played: an English gentleman stranded upon Antipodean shores. A member of the London Psychic Club with letters to prove it, come to share his expertise with others similarly interested – those who could pay, anyway.

And Muriel Nelson certainly could, and would.

Kenneth Nelson, Muriel's new husband, was younger than her, but his sleepy look had nothing to do with his expensive suit and brilliantined hair. Evie had been told he was a spoiled gigolo. She guessed he was only here tonight for the fun of it.

Diana Ashman was a brunette about the same age as her hostess. Amused and worldly, she was a famous film star, or had been a year ago when "Bushland Lady" was made. The way she sat, with a glass in one hand and a cigarette in the other, was obviously a pose. And with her crossed legs showing large expanses of flesh-coloured stockings held up by black garters, she was clearly after attention. What type of attention was also clear when she gave Daniel a sultry smile and ignored Evie.

Leo Grieves, standing behind Diana, was in his late forties, big and hearty, with thick wavy fair hair and large hands. When he moved forward to shake Daniel's hand, Evie noticed that he walked with an unmistakable limp. He turned and caught her staring. 'Miss Woodward,' he said, and swallowed her hand with his warm one. His blue gaze slid over her face, and lifted the veil. When he stepped back he did not look away.

'And this is Adele Browning, our very own avia-trix!' Muriel gushed. Adele, it turned out, had been up in an aeroplane three times but was determined to fly solo one day. She wanted to make an epic flight, as Bert Hinkler had done earlier in the year when he flew from England to Australia.

Robertson Coleman was the senior editor of the *Melbourne Clarion*. A small man with round frameless glasses, he seemed out of his depth in this company. His wife Celia, younger and prettier, was lapping up the attentions of Kenneth Nelson like a greedy kitten.

'Well.' Muriel took a deep breath. She was nervous, Evie realised. Excitement and fear were a heady mix. 'I think we're ready if you are, Mr Roxburgh? Or would you prefer a drink first?'

There was a rounded walnut cocktail cabinet against the far wall, the doors open to display a bewildering array of bottles. Nearby a lamp stood on a glass table, the bronze statue of a naked woman with arms that held aloft a glowing beach ball.

'Thank you.' Daniel smiled. 'Whisky.'

'Miss Woodward?' Muriel raised thinly plucked eyebrows.

Daniel answered for her. 'Miss Woodward doesn't drink alcohol.'

Muriel laughed shrilly. 'An abstainer! I'm afraid I couldn't do without my little drink. Thank God the wowsers haven't managed to stop us drinking in our own homes yet!'

'Muriel,' murmured Robertson Coleman, 'do remember that some of our most important advertisers belong to the temperance movement.'

'Oh, for God's sake, I can speak my mind in my own home, can't I? I'm sure Daniel agrees with me. Don't you, Daniel?'

Daniel had followed her to the cabinet. He smiled politely, hesitated, and then stopped. He stood frowning at a spot on the African rug. Muriel, turning with his glass in her hand, watched him, puzzled.

'I'm awfully sorry,' Daniel murmured, 'but it's terribly cold just here. Quite clammy.' He looked up and met Evie's eyes. 'Do you feel it, Miss Woodward?'

Evie approached him cautiously, as if feeling her way in the dark. She tensed when she reached the spot, clasping her arms about herself as if with a sudden chill.

'I *do* feel it, Mr Roxburgh. Something has happened here. Something tragic.'

Muriel Nelson dropped the glass. It bounced on the rug and rolled against the sofa. Diana Ashman rose quickly, smoothing her short skirt over slender thighs, and slid a thin supporting arm around her friend's shoulders. Far from expressing concern, she seemed to be struggling not to laugh out loud.

'Howard died there!' Muriel's eyes were as brilliant as the diamonds in her long-drop earrings. 'My first husband. Two years ago. A heart attack. Right there, on that very spot. Oh, how marvellous!'

One might almost have thought she was glad Howard was dead. Evie closed her eyes and swayed slightly. She heard Daniel shush the others and could envisage the look on his face: professional and completely focused on what was happening. The others would take his lead.

'I sense a man,' Evie murmured at last, and heard someone catch their breath. 'A large man. He's angry.' She was saying the words they had decided on, and yet somehow there really was a man. She was so engrossed in her part that he seemed to hover at the edges of her vision, vague, but vocal. She squeezed her eyes shut tight to see better. 'He says . . . he says that his wife is smoking again and she knows how he feels about that.'

Muriel clapped her hands, pulling away from her friend and reaching out for Daniel. 'That's *marvellous!* How does she do it?'

Daniel smiled. 'A gift, Mrs Nelson. A very special one.' But the glance he gave Evie said, *Be careful. Don't overdo it.*

'Does he tell you anything more?' Muriel demanded.

Evie hesitated. The fat man was still there and still angry. She closed her mind to him, forcing him back into the shadows. Imagination, it was all imagination. Daniel had done the research on Muriel Jones-Nelson: photographs, dossiers, facts and rumour. Evie probably knew more about Muriel than she did herself.

'He says that he's happy and he doesn't want you to grieve for him. He's leaving now . . . He's gone.'

Diana Ashman smirked. 'Howard's become an angel complete with wings? I find that rather difficult to believe.'

Muriel looked annoyed, but shrugged it off. 'What would you know about angels, Diana? I'm sure that Howard has learned to be a better person since he left us – and that is exactly what he would say now.' Struggling to control her fluctuating emotions, she drew a shaky breath.

Daniel eyed her sympathetically. 'There was something you wanted to show me, Muriel. You said in your letter.'

'Yes, yes of course.' She gave him a grateful smile.

'I wanted to show you the room upstairs. I'm sure it's haunted. Can I use that word?'

'Of course you can. You told me that one of your servants saw a child in the room, a little girl?'

'Yes, that's right. A girl in a long dress with ringlets in her hair. Old-fashioned – you know the sort of thing. It sounded most unlikely at the time, but then I heard about you from a friend and thought, well! If we have ghosts then I should investigate them.'

'Are you trained or a natural?' The voice startled Evie. She glanced up at Leo Grieves and he smiled modestly down at her. 'My mother is a great one for the spirits. Won't move an inch unless they tell her to. All hokum if you ask me.' He grimaced, realising what he had said. 'Sorry.'

Evie bit back a smile. 'I'm a natural, Mr Grieves. Mr Roxburgh and I met quite by chance, and he has helped me to understand my gift. It was fate.'

'Do you come from around here? Your face is familiar.'

'No, no I don't,' she lied.

'Have you worked with –'

'I won't answer any more questions just now, if you don't mind,' Evie murmured softly. 'It disturbs the atmosphere. I can't work without the right conditions.'

She began to follow Daniel and the others up the stairs. Adele was carrying a candle and giggling like a schoolgirl. Leo seemed to see Evie's request as reasonable and fell in behind her, climbing rather awkwardly. Evie took a deep breath, readying herself. The veil was annoying her and she wanted to throw it back and rub her eyes vigorously, but

Daniel would be furious with her if she broke the spell he had worked so hard to create.

'This is the room!' It was Muriel's voice. 'Oh, isn't this deliciously spooky?'

'Delicious, anyway,' Diana Ashman muttered and there was laughter. Daniel gave her a smile, but it was not quite enough to encourage her. She placed an elegant hand on his arm and stretched to whisper in his ear.

Pausing outside the door, Evie could smell the closeness, the warmth of their bodies about her. Perfume and hair oil, tobacco and alcohol, burning wax and perspiration. Someone breathed in her ear and she turned her head sharply, thinking it was Leo Grieves. But he was watching Daniel. At her glance Leo moved closer, his hand firm against the cold skin of her back, urging her forward.

'Come, Miss Woodward, don't be afraid,' he said with a hint of amusement. Impatient with herself, Evie stepped into the room.

It was a small, sparsely furnished bedroom and clearly not used very often. Daniel was by the window doing his 'Is-there-anybody-there?' routine. The candle threw his face into a striking combination of light and shadow and his hushed voice added to the disturbing effect.

Diana, unimpressed, plumped down on the bed and tipped her head back to drain the glass she had brought with her. Kenneth Nelson bent his oily head over her, murmuring something and his lips almost touched her cheek. Ignoring Muriel's loud 'Shhh!' Diana laughed huskily.

The spirits were waiting, with Evie, for Daniel's cue. He gave it, his voice vibrating with so much excitement even Diana Ashman stopped flirting. 'There's someone here, Miss Woodward.'

Evie stepped closer. 'Yes, there's a presence, Mr Roxburgh.' A child, she thought. A small child. It was what they had agreed upon. 'I feel it. A hand in mine. She's lonely. No one to play with, no one to talk to. That's why she follows the servants around.' The information should have evoked some sympathy at least, but as Evie surveyed the bored, cynical faces of Muriel Nelson's friends, she knew that dead children, no matter how lonely, were of no interest to them.

The fat man leapt back into her mind with a will of his own. Suddenly it was as if she had learned her part so completely that she had become him. Howard Jones with his shiny red face and thinning hair combed back so that each strand was visible against his speckled scalp. He was vain and powerful. And he was angry. Evie could no longer contain him.

'Muriel,' she gasped in a voice she hardly recognised. 'Muriel, this is Howard.'

Everyone froze – their eyes and mouths open. Daniel took a step towards her. His voice was low and careful. 'What do you want, Mr Jones? We're listening.'

Evie rudely turned her back on him and advanced on Muriel. 'Listen to me!' she shouted. 'I said *listen*. Two years I've been dead – two bloody years – and you're already all to hell. It was bad enough you having that slimy bastard in your bed, Muriel. Yes, that was bad enough. But did you have to go and marry him? For Christ's sake, he'll bleed you dry!'

Muriel let out a half-scream and slipped to the

floor in a dead faint.

'That's quite enough!' Robertson Coleman edged forward, pink with shock and embarrassment.

'Hello, Robertson,' Evie drawled, her voice deepening. 'Useless as ever, I see. Your career is in the shit and you're taking my newspaper with it. No one respects you anymore, not even your wife. Christ, I wish I'd given you the boot before I died!'

The little man stumbled back, silenced. Everyone was watching Evie and waiting as she stood trembling before them. Diana Ashman looked up from where she was tending Muriel. Her pale eyes glittered oddly and she glared at Evie as if she really was seeing the newspaper tycoon's image. 'Well,' she said softly, 'this certainly has turned out to be an interesting evening. Have you anything to tell *me,* Howard? Don't stint yourself, now; you never did when you were alive.'

Evie laughed savagely. 'Why should I bother to tell you anything? You know what you are. You all know what you are: leeches, syphoning my fortune into your own greedy bellies. I didn't work twenty hours a day so that you and your kind could spend my money! Bastards, the lot of you. Bastards!' Spittle sprayed out of her mouth.

Daniel stood behind her. 'Miss Woodward!' It was a command. He wanted Evie to stop, but she didn't seem able to.

'You'll be sorry,' Howard Jones's deep, angry voice vibrated in her throat. 'You think you can do as you like and get away with it. Well, you bloody can't. There's a reckoning on the way. A reckoning!'

Cold fingers closed on her arm and their long

nails scratched her bare skin. She shuddered, and Howard Jones vanished in an instant as something else began to seep into her head: smoke from a damp, sulky fire. It drifted, formed shapes, grew a voice. Shocked and terrified, Evie swayed and would have fallen if Daniel hadn't grabbed her.

'*Au secours,* Evangeline,' a voice whispered. *Help me, Evangeline.* '*Voulez-vous m'aider?*' *Could you help me?*

CHAPTER 2

'YOU TOOK A RISK.'

Muriel couldn't wait for them to go and now Daniel was annoyed with her. Evie wound down the window and let the breeze stir her fair hair. The veil had been discarded as soon as they had left Muriel. The enigmatic Miss Evangeline Woodward had given way to Mrs Evie Rose, widow and mother.

'Why did you tell her all that stuff? I've explained to you that people like to believe the dear departed are in a state of grace. Even the meanest bastards turn into angels when they die.'

Evie shrugged, determined that Daniel would not see her inner disquiet. Her memories of her performance were vague but there was a shivery sense of dread, a feeling that she had opened a box that would have been better left closed.

'You've probably put them off.'

'They were impressed. Being insulted by Howard Jones meant more to them than the ghost of a little girl with ringlets. I saw the way it was and I made a decision. There wasn't time to warn you.'

He snorted. 'You're a good actress, I'll give you

that, but even good actresses make mistakes.'

'I don't.' Evie had had enough practice playing a part in her life to feel confident that she rarely got it wrong.

'You were lucky this time.'

'I'm always lucky,' she retorted. 'And we got away with it, didn't we?' She let amusement creep into her voice. 'Stop fussing, Daniel. They loved us.'

He glanced at her as he turned the car into a smaller, meaner street. 'You know it worries me when you start sounding like me.'

Negotiating the kerb, he turned again, into another street of dull windows. Earle Street. Daniel stopped and there was complete silence in the car. Evie looked about bleakly. Maybe it was the contact with houses like Muriel Nelson's. If she hadn't seen the way the other half lived, maybe she wouldn't have noticed how awful her present home was. With a sigh, she asked, 'Why does night always seem darker here?'

Daniel put a gold lighter engraved with his initials to his cigarette. 'Lack of street lights,' he said simply. 'Is Gwen home?'

Evie peered along the street at number 5. The curtain in the front sitting room glowed. Gwen would be there, waiting, knitting. Gwen knitted regardless of the weather. 'She's there. She's minding Jimmy for me.'

'Maybe I should call in on her one day.'

Was he joking? It didn't sound like it. Evie watched him uneasily. 'You know that's not a good idea, Daniel. You know how she feels about you. If she knew I was working for you she'd have a fit. I told her I was going out tonight with Dolly.'

Daniel exhaled the smoke thoughtfully. 'You mean Dolly your non-existent friend from the non-existent clothing shop where you work?'

He made the lie seem worse and Evie felt the need to justify herself.

'I couldn't tell her the truth.'

'No, you couldn't do that.' There was no emotion in his voice and yet she sensed the hurt. Since when had Daniel cared what Gwen thought about him?

'Daniel,' she sighed. 'If she knew I was working for you there'd be trouble. I don't want to upset her because she's been good to me. She's been through enough.'

He continued smoking in silence. The past lay between them, thick as molasses. Evie refused to be caught up in its sticky strands and let the moment pass. Instead she turned her head and stared out of the car window.

Earle Street had lost much of its respectability in recent years. It had once been a good area, but now those with the money to move out had done so. There were 'To Let' signs up and down the block, and a sly grog shop on the corner, where drinkers not content with the six o'clock closing law went to pass the otherwise long, dry nights. Members of the push had begun roaming the lanes, fighting among themselves or threatening pedestrians – Mrs Higgins's son had been beaten for refusing to hand over a bag of tomatoes. Gwen said it wasn't like this even five years ago. You didn't see broken fences, unpainted houses and squalid yards then. Poverty and unemployment were growing like a dark shadow, creeping across the city; and Evie had no intention of being swallowed up by it.

Hence Daniel – and the lies.

Evie had lived at number 5 Earle Street with Gwen's son Billy after they were married. It was the house Billy had grown up in and was across the street from Daniel's. Billy and Daniel had been best friends when they were young, although Gwen said now that she'd never liked Daniel. She blamed him for Billy's death; she seemed to need someone to blame.

Evie blamed Earle Street. After Billy died she made up her mind that she wasn't going to stay here. She would save up and when she had enough money she was going to move herself and Jimmy and Gwen to somewhere better. At times her responsibilities frightened her and she wondered whether she could really pull it off. Then she would remember Billy. The least she could do was look after his son and his mother, as he would have done, even if it meant taking part in Daniel Roxburgh's scams. The fact that she was enjoying herself – or had been until this evening – didn't really come into it.

'Evie?'

Daniel was watching her. Mentally she shook herself; she was tired.

'Where did all that stuff come from tonight?'

She eyed him slyly. Where had it come from? How could she tell him that it was all tied up with things in her past that she had no intention of allowing him to rifle through? Things she had no intention of reliving.

'Evie?'

'The spirit of Howard Jones really did possess me

tonight, Daniel,' she said cheerfully.

He frowned and tossed his cigarette out of the car window. 'Just don't let it happen again.'

She laughed and moved to open her door, but he wasn't ready to let her go yet.

'What did you think of Leo Grieves?'

'Think of him?' She collected her thoughts, sorting Leo out from the other guests. 'He was polite. He said he thought he knew my face and I don't think it was a line. Why?'

'He was in France during the war. I'm surprised you haven't heard of him. He has a medal for bravery.'

'He's a hero then, like you?'

'Yeah.' He half-smiled at the old joke. 'Comes from a rich family. His brother makes moving pictures. Gwen's probably heard of *him*. There's a mansion on the bay, the lot. More money than you could even imagine.'

'I don't know. I could imagine a lot. Is the mansion haunted, do you think?'

He laughed softly, a warm sound that set off a warning in her head. She tensed. He reached out and brushed a finger lightly across the strap at her shoulder. 'Did I tell you that you look quite exquisite in that get-up, old girl?' he mocked.

She smiled back, pretending to be unaffected, while her stomach twisted. Daniel leaned forward suddenly as if he was going to kiss her. She stiffened and pulled back, pressing herself to the door like, she grimaced afterwards, a virgin under attack.

He got the message. 'Goodnight, Evie,' he said coolly. 'I'll see you in a day or two. We need to discuss our next case.' As if he was a detective, he always called them 'cases'.

'Yes. Of course.' Evie felt foolish now and embarrassed and then angry at herself for being so. Daniel probably kissed all his lady friends – she didn't have to make such a fuss about it. 'Goodnight, Daniel,' she said.

It wasn't until she reached number 5, unlocked the door and closed it behind her that she heard his car drive away. She sighed and, propping a hand against the wall, slipped off her new shoes. In his way Daniel watched out for her, just as Billy had done. Only whereas Billy had been such a clear character – as clear as water – Daniel was all shadows – she touched her lips and sighed again. She didn't really know Daniel; she never had. And since Billy had died, she seemed to be removed from men in general, as if there was a sheet of glass between her and the everyday world.

Had that been her doing, or had the fact that she was a young widow still grieving for her dead husband made other men wary of becoming too friendly with her? Of course when it came to Daniel, there were other things that complicated their relationship: Billy's memory and the fact that he was Daniel's best friend, their joint loyalty to Billy, and Gwen's dislike of Daniel. And then there was Billy's son, Jimmy.

The fact that Billy and Daniel had been best friends should have made it easier, but it didn't. And Evie was not sure exactly why that was, unless it was because it was Daniel who Evie had met first. She had been Daniel's girl, in a way.

Two years earlier Daniel had had a job as the manager of a dance hall called the Grande Ballroom, a scruffy barn of a place not quite in St Kilda. Like Daniel, it had a reputation. Evie had gone there one night with a friend and Daniel had rescued her from a desperate situation – she had been grateful for that. He was a handsome man, smart and interesting, although she had always felt slightly out of her depth with him. 'Here's my hero!' she had said, whenever she saw him after the Grande Ballroom, and they'd laughed and joked. But Evie had never regarded him as a serious romantic prospect; she had never felt as if she knew him well enough for that, not properly.

It was Daniel who subsequently introduced her to Billy, and Billy was the one she had come to see as her great love and salvation. She had never made any secret of that.

'I want you to meet my friend,' Daniel had told her that fateful day. 'Billy Rose. He still lives in Earle Street. You'll like Billy; everyone does.'

She *had* liked Billy. There was an obvious attraction between them from the first. But, more than that, she had fallen in love with Billy Rose in a single afternoon.

Daniel had had someone to visit in the area, one of his shady friends, and had left her in the Earle Street house. Billy and Gwen had made her comfortable in the front room with all its threadbare middle-class pretensions. Billy, with his blue eyes and sweet face, and Gwen hanging around him over-protectively.

Billy had spoken about Daniel. He had told Evie that Daniel had lived in the house opposite, that his mother was dead now, that his father had been dead for years and that Daniel and he had been best mates for as long as either of them could remember.

Gwen, disliking Daniel as she did, had told Evie how he had been in trouble with the police in his younger days. Although the mistake of being caught hadn't been repeated, some of his more recent jobs had been in a grey area when it came to the law. In contrast, according to Gwen, Billy had led a predictably blameless life. He was working as a foreman in a farm machinery factory, not a particularly well paid job, but an honest one.

'Mum,' Billy sighed, and gave Evie a look that said: *She loves me. Forgive her.* 'Daniel's the smartest bloke I know.' It was clear that he wasn't just saying it; he really did admire Daniel, but he didn't want to *be* Daniel. The two of them had always been friends and, despite what Gwen thought, they were similar in many ways. But Evie didn't love Daniel. She loved Billy.

By the time Daniel returned to number 5, Evie Woodward had made her decision. Her future lay with Billy Rose.

Afterwards, Daniel had made a joke of it. 'You stole my girl,' he'd laugh. And Billy would laugh back and say, 'Just proves that the hero doesn't always get the girl.' But Daniel and Billy were friends and always would be. Daniel came to the wedding, sent a present when Jimmy was born, and attended Billy's funeral. To Evie he was polite, complimentary and sympathetic, in that order. He kept his distance. It was not until recently that she had spoken to him again – properly, anyway.

Three months ago, she had stepped off a tram and Daniel was standing at the stop. She had felt awkward but, in his smart dark suit and shiny shoes, he had not been content with a few polite words. It was cold, threatening rain, and Evie had just lost her latest job in a match factory and didn't expect to get another again soon.

There was less and less work as the 1920s drew to an end; the number of men applying at the town hall for employment was frightening, and who knew how many women were out of work? Gwen's age and arthritis left her unfit for work and Evie had found only the occasional short term job here and there, with little pay. She was beginning to feel like the last chocolate in the box, the one that nobody wanted. And then along came Daniel – handsome, smiling Daniel. He caught her at a weak moment.

Against her better judgment, Evie had let him take her to a café for tea and sultana cake – sultana cake was always her favourite. They sat down at a window table, snug inside the steamy warmth while outside the wind blew and passers-by shivered. Daniel began to tell her that he had a scheme to make lots of money and go west. 'Perth,' he said and winked. 'No one knows me there. I fancy the idea of that, no one knowing me. Sometimes Melbourne can be a bloody small town.'

It all sounded familiar. Gwen would say that Daniel was in trouble again and that he had to get away.

Like a fool, she'd asked, 'What scheme is that, Daniel?'

He'd told her. It sounded harmless, the way he told it anyway, a bit of fun, and play-acting. These days, he'd said, people paid to go to the pictures and see make-believe. Why not get them to pay for Daniel to bring it to their own homes?

Evie picked up a stray sultana off her plate and popped it into her mouth. It was time for her to return to the real world. But reluctant to leave the warmth, the sound of Daniel's voice and the fantasy he was weaving for her, she didn't move.

'I need a partner.' He met her startled gaze blandly. 'She'd have to be able to put on a front – an act – and she'd have to be beautiful enough to keep the punters from thinking straight.'

Evie frowned down at her empty cup. 'She?' she ventured.

'You,' he said.

She laughed and spread out her arms as if to say, *Me? Look at me, Daniel!*

He looked at her. There was a hole in her stocking and her dress was damp at the hem and stained from her work in the factory. Her hair had come out of its pins and hung lank about her face. She looked pale. Her eyes were tired with the strain of trying to earn enough money to keep Billy's house and his family going. At twenty-four she would soon look ten years older.

'Why not?' he asked her. 'You're the one I want, Evie. You know about rich people and their houses. You've got class and you know how to act the lady. I'll get you new clothes, whatever you need. I'll pay you more than any shop or factory around here could dream of. You'll soon have enough money to do whatever you want.'

Get out of Earle Street was her immediate thought, but she shut the door on it. 'Billy would have hated me doing what you're saying.'

'Billy would have lived and died in the same house, in the same street, with Gwen making him the same sandwiches every morning to take to a job he hated. Oh, I know he was the salt of the earth and all that —'

'If you say anything against Billy, I'll walk out right now!'

'I wasn't!' He lowered his voice as the other customers turned to stare and the girl behind the counter, her bleached hair tortured into tight, shiny waves, glared. 'I'm not saying anything bad. Billy was my mate, you know that. I would've done anything for him. Given him anything —' He looked at her hard. 'I did. He had you and I let him have you.'

Evie shifted uncomfortably in her chair. 'You make it sound as if you and I were . . . together. That wasn't the case, Daniel. We were friends; that was all.'

'We still are, I hope,' he retorted lightly.

He repeated his plans, binding her again in his spell. With Daniel anything seemed possible, even the impossible. Gradually any objections she had to his scheme faded, and the voice in her head, Billy's voice, which kept saying *No, no, no,* was drowned by her own voice. And it said, *Why not?*

Gwen was knitting. The wireless was playing, but the click of her needles was louder. Her hands were twisted with arthritis, but that didn't seem to stop her. She liked to be useful, she said. A widow herself for twenty years, she was used to being alone and her knitting kept her company.

'Evie,' she said and smiled. Her face was creased and softened with wrinkles but she had Billy's blue eyes. 'I thought I'd wait up, just in case,' she said.

Evie didn't ask in case of what. She sank down into a threadbare armchair. It was hot and stuffy and she longed for a cool breeze. 'Was little Jimmy good?'

'Like an angel.'

'Oh, Gwen, he's anything but that.' Getting on for a year old now, Jimmy was into everything.

'Nonsense. He's been as good as gold. How was your evening, love?'

Evie kept smiling with some effort. 'That Dolly can dance!'

There was a fond gleam in Gwen's eye and she laughed. 'I don't mind you enjoying yourself, love. You work so hard at the dress shop, you deserve it.' She put her knitting aside. 'Tell me about it.'

Evie started to tell a fictitious version of her evening. As far as Gwen knew, she worked at a posh dress shop with Dolly, a shop where the owner was willing to hand out clothing to the girls so that they would look the part and bring in new customers. Dolly had grown into quite a character over the weeks and Gwen couldn't wait to meet her. Evie had so far managed to make Dolly's excuses believable, but there would come a day when she and Dolly would have to have a serious falling out.

'It's a long time since I went dancing,' Gwen said. 'None of this Charleston nonsense then. We waltzed.' Peter Dawson's mellow baritone drifted out of the wireless and Gwen's sigh turned into a smile. 'Listen! Don't you love him? I don't know

how you managed to find the money for that con-
traption, Evie, and you shouldn't have spent it on
me, but I get that much pleasure from it!'

Evie smiled and let her rattle on, only catching
a word here and there. Gwen had recently been
to a matinee with her neighbour, Vi Morgan, to
share a box of Old Gold chocolates and watch
Rudolph Valentino, their favourite actor, in "A
Sainted Devil". The fact that Valentino had been
dead for two years only seemed to increase his
appeal. Gwen and Vi constantly bemoaned the fact
that now there were talking pictures – "The Jazz
Singer" had been shown in America – and they'd
never hear Valentino's voice.

'– Billy.'

Evie lifted her head. Gwen was smiling at her,
pleased with what she'd said. She laughed when
she realised that Evie hadn't heard a word.

'I said Vi read my tea leaves. She said she saw
Billy in them.'

'What did Billy say?' Evie didn't set much store
by Vi Morgan's tea leaf readings.

'He didn't say anything. Vi told me his spirit's
watching over us. Isn't that a comforting thought?'

'Very.'

'Daniel was there, too.' She twitched irritably.
'He's a bad lot. He killed Billy, and I told Vi too.
I remember when the police came for him that
time, how his mother cried. The Squizzy Taylor
of Earle Street, that's what he was – a proper little gangster. His mother's better off dead and not
knowing what she gave birth to.'

Evie felt compelled to say, 'Billy believed it was
the company Daniel was keeping at the time.'

Gwen shrugged her shoulders. 'Billy always made excuses for Daniel. Pretty ironic to me that his so-called friend killed him.'

'Gwen,' Evie murmured, 'please. It was Billy's idea to work an hour later, not Daniel's.'

'But it was Daniel's fault!' Gwen's chin stuck out. 'If he hadn't been with Daniel he wouldn't have *had* to work an hour later!'

'He didn't know he'd see Daniel that day; it was just chance. A coincidence.'

Gwen gave her a look. 'Sounds like you're on his side.'

'No, of course I'm not! I just want to be fair. Daniel and Billy were friends.'

'And Daniel brought you here that day to meet Billy.'

Evie laughed off the sudden suspicious gleam in her mother-in-law's eyes. 'Then I should thank him with all my heart.' The laugh went awry. 'Billy wouldn't have blamed Daniel, Gwen; you know that. You know how he was. Sometimes I think if only . . .'

Gwen reached out and took her hand, the bitterness forgotten. 'Never mind, love. That Daniel's not worth our arguing over. I'm glad you and Dolly had a good night.'

For a moment they sat in silence and then Evie stood up and a yawn slipped through her smile. 'I'm sorry, I have to go to bed,' she said.

'Of course you do, love. All that dancing! Goodnight, Evie.'

Little Jimmy was asleep in his cot. The faintest of breezes came through the open window. Evie slipped off the black dress and hung it in the wardrobe with the blue one Daniel had bought her last time, and the coffee one the time before that. She sat at her dressing table and began to brush her hair.

As if they had been waiting, tonight's memories came swooping down upon her. Howard Jones and his filthy tongue, Muriel's face, and the other guests, shocked and excited. Everything had gone to plan – well, almost everything. Maybe she had allowed matters to get out of hand, just a little bit, but everything had been fine until the end . . . Howard Jones had never, to Evie's knowledge, spoken in French.

Evie shuddered as her thoughts slid deeper, into the past she never spoke of. She had left all that behind her, years before – hadn't she? Then how could it sneak up on her now and frighten her so? She wished that Billy was here. His solid common sense would have restored her equilibrium. Billy had been her anchor. Evie had clung to him as if, without him, she might simply float away. Now there was only Billy's family to hold on to, and sometimes the responsibility of that seemed almost too much for her to bear.

What about Daniel? a voice in her head reminded her.

Daniel, she thought, and put the brush down. Daniel was Billy's friend, that's what he was. Anything else was out of the question.

'*Au secours, Evangeline,*' she whispered aloud, and shuddered again. *Help me.* The face in the shadowy mirror, framed by fair hair so soft and loose, was a stranger's face. She had a sense of dislocation. The past was strong. Evie, the child whose girlhood was a fractured puzzle, refused to be thrust aside. Her earliest memories were mainly to do with her father, that domineering man, and her frightened mother. Her childhood had ended abruptly when she turned fourteen, and the Frenchwoman had come into her life.

And after that? Running, hiding, vague recollections of rented rooms and the jobs her mother couldn't keep. Then a long period of stability, when she had worked as a maid for a family who were kind to her.

Her mother had died in 1925 and Evie had left her job. Something had brought her back here to Melbourne and she had found work in the Peking Tea Rooms for long hours and not much pay. Then the fateful night of the Grande Ballroom and Daniel. Through Daniel she had met Billy and found happiness, but it had been cruelly taken from her. And now it was as if those long ago days were returning, as if the play-acting she had been doing with Daniel had somehow drawn them up from the dark well where they had been hiding.

Her mother had always said that it was best to keep walking forward and never, ever look back. Evie had tried to do just that, but now it seemed as if the choice was being taken out of her hands.

She slipped beneath the sheet and lay still. Outside voices rose and fell as customers for the sly grog shop passed by. She closed her eyes. When she was young and had been so unhappy she had dreamed of a home of her own, a place of love and safety. So far this was the closest she had come to it. Not the house itself, not Earle Street, but what the house contained. Gwen and the baby and her memories of Billy. She had to hang on to all that; she had to work towards keeping it.

The baby turned and made a soft snuffling sound. Evie held her breath, listening, but he slipped back into sleep and, after a moment, Evie slept too.

CHAPTER 3

Dearest Evie
Will you meet me at the shop tomorrow?
I have something to tell you.
Dolly

EVIE SMILED WRYLY AS SHE remembered the note that had arrived at the door last evening and been placed in Gwen's eager hand. She had been angry at the time, thinking Gwen must have known it was written by Daniel, but Gwen hadn't.

'I'm glad you have a friend like Dolly,' was all she had said. 'Of course you must see her. I'll watch Jimmy.'

Guilt had eaten at Evie, but still she'd agreed. And she'd gone.

The 'shop' was Daniel's office in Little Lonsdale Street. A doorway led in off the footpath and an old cable tram rumbled across the intersection with Swanston Street as Evie began to climb the grimy steps. A man was clattering down the staircase towards her. As he came closer she recognised one of Daniel's flashily dressed friends. He tipped his hat, grinned at her, and then was gone out onto the street, a black Gladstone bag clasped tightly in his meaty hand.

Daniel's door was newly painted with a sign that said *The Roxburgh Psychic Detective Agency.* In the beginning he had considered calling himself a spirit hunter, but Evie had laughed and told him that it made him sound like a member of the Temperance Movement rather than a ghostly investigator.

She knocked and walked in.

Despite the open window the office was hot, and she could hear the sounds drifting up from the street below. Not many clients came here. Daniel discouraged them. The pokey room was used more as a storage area for his files and a place he could work on his cases and pick up his mail than as a place for consultations. The big desk wouldn't have looked out of place in the late Howard Jones's office, but the rest of the furniture was tatty and obviously secondhand. Evie noted that the leather sofa had a pillow at one end – evidence of Daniel's current domestic arrangements. She always made a point of not asking him about his private life.

With what appeared to be an effort, Daniel gave her a half-smile and tossed some folders he had been looking through into a heap on the desk. A spare shirt was draped over the back of his chair, a shaving mug and razor laid out on a towel.

'You're early,' he said shortly.

'Sorry. Did I interrupt?' It hadn't occurred to her that she might be interrupting him, although Daniel always had some deal or other going. It was part of being Daniel Roxburgh. But this morning he looked . . . tired. Less than enthusiastic.

'No,' he said. 'You didn't interrupt. It was nothing important.' His shirt was sweaty, the buttons open to half-way down so that it hung open as he bent over. His trousers had obviously been slept in, too, his hair was untidy and he had yet to make use of the shaving gear. He was less than his usual polished self.

The idea gnawed at her. She was not used to thinking of Daniel as someone who might need careful treatment or a bit of consideration. Someone who might have a bad day just like everyone else.

'Sit down,' he said, brushing a hand over the cracked leather sofa, as if it had to be perfect before he would allow her to use it. 'I'll put the fan on. Do you want a drink?'

'Water, thanks.' The electric fan rattled, stirring the air in the room like a spoon in a pot of soup. He poured her a glass of water and returned to his desk. She noticed then that he already had a tumbler quarter-filled with whisky, while a second glass had been emptied by himself. Or his visitor.

The man with the Gladstone bag.

'Who was it just left?' she asked, smoothing her skirt over her knees. 'I recognised the face but I've forgotten the name. Was he one of Connor's men?'

Gunner Connor was a local standover man and someone Daniel knew well.

Now Daniel gave her a look and she wished she hadn't asked. After a moment he said, 'Don't worry about that. I've got something to show you.'

Evie took the newspaper cutting he held out to her. It was from the *Melbourne Clarion* of two days ago. There was a headline, "Former Newspaper Owner Speaks!" Underneath was an amusing description of the evening at Muriel Nelson's house – certainly more amusing than the evening itself had been. Howard Jones's nasty return from the grave had been given an entirely different slant. Evie chuckled as she read it, easily recognising herself and Daniel, and thinking herself lucky that Gwen didn't take the *Clarion*. The article gave no indication that the journalist thought the experience authentic or anything more than an entertaining interlude.

'The dashing Mr Roxburgh and his lovely assistant,' she read. 'We sound like a magic act.'

There was one short paragraph tacked on: a quote from a local vicar well known for his opposition to Spiritualism.

He called for a halt to 'these antics' and denounced Daniel as a charlatan.

Evie raised her eyebrows. 'Is this good for us, Daniel? I don't know if I like being denounced.'

'I've had five new enquiries already.'

She smiled back. 'Good, then.'

He picked up an envelope from a pile on the desk. 'Including this one from Leo Grieves.'

'Leo Grieves the war hero?'

'The very same.' He tapped the envelope, turning it end over end.

'With all the money?'

'And the mansion on the bay.'

'What does he want?'

Daniel opened the letter. 'It's not so much what *Leo* wants. His mother requires "a full and thorough psychic investigation of Blue Waters". That's the name of the mansion on the bay, by the way.

Blue Waters.'

The glass slipped out of Evie's hand. Water ran down her yellow dress, soaking her stockings and her shoes. Her mind was blank. Nothing. A blue nothingness, perfectly even in colour, with no shades or lighter patches. Periwinkle blue. Blue like the sky. Blue like Billy's eyes. *Au secours,* a far away voice whispered. *Help me, Evangeline.* But she knew she couldn't. She couldn't help. She hadn't been able to help when she was fourteen and she didn't know how to help now.

'Evie!' Daniel was gripping her hands. He sounded frantic. She stared back at him as the blue slowly faded. She blinked and understanding returned. She grimaced and looked down at where the water had spilt. Her dress had a damp patch. The insides of her shoes felt wet.

Daniel let her go. 'Here,' he handed her the shirt which had been hanging over the back of his chair. She began to mop at herself to sop up the worst of the damage. 'Are you all right?'

She unbuckled her shoes and shook out droplets of water. 'Apart from being wet, yes.'

'What was it?'

She laughed, refusing to meet his eyes. 'I spilt my water, Daniel,' she said, and dropped the shirt onto the floor. 'There, that'll do.'

'Do you want another glass?'

Evie shook her head in self-mockery. 'No, Daniel, I do not!'

He sat down beside her. His shirt was still unbuttoned and she could see the warm shadows of his chest, the dark sprinkling of hair, the lean muscle. Something inside her locked, like a car's wheels on a slippery road. A memory surfaced – of her hands on Billy's chest, of her lips following the dips and curves. Except that now it was Daniel's chest in her mind, not Billy's, and the sensation of Daniel's warm skin under her hands. That was wrong, surely. She shouldn't be thinking about Daniel like that. The hum of the fan seemed suddenly loud. She looked away.

But he'd noticed. He'd gone very still. 'What was it, Evie?' he repeated quietly.

What was it? Her mind cringed at the question. First the voice, the seductive French voice, and now the sheet of blue, filling every corner of her mind. Both had been part of *before,* the past. She did not dare imagine what all of this meant. How could she tell Daniel what she didn't understand herself?

'I miss Billy,' she said, the first thing that came to mind.

He seemed taken aback, but gave his answer easily enough. 'So do I.'

'He worked an hour later than usual,' she murmured, as if she hadn't heard him. 'If he hadn't been there, he wouldn't have died. Some other man would have been standing there instead when that crate fell. All because he met you and stayed talking and then he had to make up the time.'

He leaned back against the sofa and stared up at the smoke-stained ceiling.

'Gwen blames you, of course.'

'Of course.'

'They didn't let me see him, did you know that? They said he'd been crushed and it was better that I didn't see. They thought *they* knew what was best for me. I wanted to see him, though. I needed to. Sometimes I wonder if maybe it wasn't him and that he isn't really dead. Could it have been some-one else, Daniel? Could Billy be alive, somewhere?'

'Evie, please. You know he's dead. Billy's dead. He's been dead for nearly a year.'

'And Gwen blames you.'

He closed his eyes. There was a nerve ticking in his cheek. 'Do you think I wouldn't have stopped it happening if I could have? I couldn't see the future that day and neither could Billy. We talked about football, for Christ's sake. We had a joke or two. We promised to catch up another day. It was nothing.'

'It seems such a small thing, doesn't it? But that hour meant Billy's death. He would never have left early, knowing he'd had extra time off for lunch. He was always going to make it up at the end of the day. That was Billy.'

Daniel groaned. 'Come here.' He put his arms around her and pulled her against him. She closed her eyes and breathed in perspiration and whisky and all the more subtle scents that were his. His chest moved with each breath. This was the closest she had been to him since the night of the Grande Ballroom. Even at Billy's funeral he had done no more than take her hand.

'Sometimes I think it was my fault,' she said against his shirt. 'If I hadn't married him he would have been all right. I was selfish and I wanted to live an ordinary life, and I chose Billy.'

'And why is that your fault?'

'Because – it is.'

You're a bad girl, Evie. A wicked, lying girl. She knew the voice in her head: it was her father's, and it had done its work well. In her grimer moments she still believed that Billy had died because she hadn't been good enough for him, hadn't loved him enough, hadn't been unselfish enough. But Daniel didn't need to know that.

The feel of him so close to her, the stroke of his hand in her hair, was making her a little dizzy, like too much champagne. Her mouth curved in a self-derisory smile – this wasn't exactly keeping him at arm's length.

'Look,' he said now, 'if you don't want to take on Leo Grieves, that's all right. I'll think of something.'

He sounded as if he didn't care, but she knew he was disappointed. He had to be, at the thought of losing so lucrative a client. He stroked his thumb over a spot on her back with a repeated circular caress. It made her tingle; it felt wonderful. And suddenly she was frightened. Daniel was a threat to her safe and ordinary life. He inhabited a world where nothing was ever what it seemed and the ground wasn't firm under your feet but shaky and liable to open up and swallow you. She used to live like that, so she knew how it felt. She couldn't risk drawing Jimmy and Gwen into those shadowy realms.

But neither could she risk losing this job.

'There'll be other opportunities, Evie. Take the week off. I'll give you some money. Go to the beach for a day. Buy yourself an ice cream.'

She made herself laugh. 'Wild extravagance, huh?'

He did pay her well. He might be dangerous and she might not trust him or his schemes as far as she could throw them, but he was helping her in ways no one else could. She thought now of her growing bank account and reminded herself what that money could mean for her and Gwen and Jimmy. Soon she would begin to make enquiries about renting a house in a better area, or maybe even buying. Leaving Earle Street with its growing incidence of nightly assaults behind. Jimmy would grow up without seeing drunken men reel home from the grog shop or louts intent on violence.

She sat up and straightened her yellow cloche hat. She felt cold without his arms around her but she ignored the feeling, just as she had learned to ignore all waves on her smooth sea. To Evie the weather was always calm, and if there was a storm brooding over the horizon she refused to see it.

'Tell me about Blue Waters, Daniel.' She had made her decision.

He could not hide his relief. 'If you're sure – ?'

'I am.'

He began slowly, dredging up the relevant information. 'Leo Grieves's father was Sir Henry Grieves. He made his fortune on the Bendigo goldfields. He was a millionaire when he died aged 82 in 1912. I remember hearing about him when I was a kid – his reputation was less than savoury.'

'Why?' she asked.

He began to button his shirt. 'He spent money on his house, but not much on anything else. Ruthless was his middle name. He kept his employees hungry – said they worked better on empty stomachs. He was an old goat when it came to women, too. Couldn't leave them alone. That was how he met his second wife, Leo's mother.'

'She was one of his servants.' How did she know that? She tried to remember what else she might have heard of Sir Henry Grieves but couldn't. There was nothing. Her mind was like a book with the relevant pages torn out and the realisation was a disturbing one – but not unknown to her.

'Blue Waters *was* Sir Henry Grieves,' Daniel went on. 'His ghost must be a permanent resident. A few good lines for you there, wouldn't you say?'

'Yes, I suppose so. I'll work on them.'

'Good girl. Let's make the most of this while it lasts. One day we'll go out of fashion, just like penny-farthings.'

Evie raised her eyebrows. 'Are penny-farthings out of fashion?' she asked with a twinkle in her eye.

He laughed, got to his feet and turned away to search the drawers of the desk for a cigarette. 'If Leo Grieves wants the full treatment, he'll get it,' he said over his shoulder.

'Was that why you sent the note? To tell me about Leo Grieves?'

Daniel found a cigarette, lit it and slipped the gold lighter back into his pocket. 'No. You're putting on a séance tomorrow night. A brother and sister called Beatson. They want to contact their mother. She made a new will before she died, hid it away somewhere, and they can't find it.'

She nodded. 'All right. Is there anything interesting I can use?'

He handed her a sheet of paper covered in his careful handwriting. She glanced at it before folding it and tucking it out of sight in her bag. 'I'll pick you up tomorrow night at the end of Earle Street,' Daniel said as she stood up.

'Around the corner, just to be on the safe side. Vi Morgan sees everything.'

'Around the corner it is, then.'

She gave him a grin. 'See you then – *Dolly.*'

There was a gleam in his eyes – half-smile and half something else. It gave her a tingle clear down to her toes. She hurried down the stairs as if Squizzy Taylor himself were behind her.

There was a man in a suit waiting at the bottom, standing there as if he had nowhere in particular to go. He was wearing a hat and his eyes were cast down, but Evie knew what he was. Not Connor's man this time, but someone from the opposing side. What did the police want with Daniel?

A tram rattled up as she reached the corner and she glanced back as she boarded it. The detective had vanished up Daniel's stairs. It wasn't anything to do with her, she reminded herself, as she found a seat. She had enough problems of her own without trying to untangle Daniel's – although he was a big part of them. Her eyes fixed on the passing street-scape, her mind mulling over what he had said just now and the way he had comforted her and the way she had felt being held in his arms. Then she thought about the blue and Blue Waters, but those thoughts were too disturbing and she pushed them aside.

Melbourne slid by in a series of stops and starts. The heat turned straight lines into shimmers and the glare of the sky flashed between the buildings. A tall man was climbing the steps of the town hall with a cane in one hand, an umbrella in the other and a bowler hat on his head. Evie's heart gave a thud. He reminded her of her father, although she did not think of him often.

And she wouldn't think of him now, but for

some reason today her mind refused to obey her. Unwelcome memories squirmed out from their dark corners.

Frederick Woodward was a valet of the old school, a gentleman's gentleman. He believed that a servant's own needs were always subordinate to the needs of the family he served. Not that Frederick had ever thought of himself as a servant. He looked down upon servants. He was the master's man and therefore a cut above the rest. And his daughter had in turn to be a step above other girls.

Evie had been educated accordingly, and taught to speak correctly, to play the piano and to sing — all the accomplishments required in a lady, for it was assumed that was what she would one day be. A proper little lady.

You're a proper little lady, aren't you?

Who had said that? Her father? She didn't think so. The voice was a buzz in her head, like a bee bumping against a dark window pane. She felt damp with perspiration. There was a handkerchief in her purse and with her fingers shaking she fumbled to open it. For just a moment there was something at the edge of her mind. Something dark and enormous, waiting to pounce.

And then it was gone.

Her father had been a tall man, always impeccably dressed, with his shoes polished, buttons shone and not a hair out of place on his grey head. He seemed barely human. His face was a stern and emotionless mask, and old. He always seemed so old. He must have been old when she was born. She could not imagine him young or smiling. He never smiled and he never laughed. He had never been the sort of father to cling to. She had read a story once about a girl who had run to greet her father and been swept up into his arms. She could not conceive of doing such a thing herself.

The handkerchief was out and she dabbed her face with it, breathing deeply. *Enough, that was enough.* She tried to turn her thoughts away, but today none of the usual tricks worked. The blue she had seen in her mind in Daniel's office had opened places that had not been opened in years and were better left closed.

You're a proper little lady, aren't you?

She pressed the handkerchief against her mouth. The sense of darkness was back, closing in on her, but now there were other feelings too. Smallness, a small enclosed space. Somewhere hidden. *Quiet, you must be very very quiet. Not a peep from you, Evangeline . . .*

Had that voice belonged to her mother? No, not her mother. Her mother had been as frightened of Frederick as she had been and even when they ran away, she had remained afraid until her dying day. Evie flinched, remembering despite herself, a familiar and unpleasant scene. She was a child standing in a doorway, peering in. Her father was seated in his favourite armchair, the cylinder player on the table at his elbow, the music coming from it. And she was being ever so quiet, so very very quiet. Because if she were to make a noise and be discovered *spying,* she would be punished. And she didn't like her father's punishments –

No!

Maybe she had said it out loud. The woman sitting in front of her turned and stared. Evie peered blindly through the window. So many faces and names, so many voices and words, a jumble in her head. A puzzle she had never been able to assemble properly. There was only pain in attempting it – a wrenching, searing pain like no other.

And then the blue. The sheet of endless blue, swallowing her whole.

Evie's stop was next and she stepped thankfully onto the footpath. The air was steamy, working up to a storm. In her yellow dress and yellow hat, she felt like a wilting sunflower. The tram trundled away behind her and other alighting passengers pushed by her, but she didn't notice.

A hairdresser's salon straddled the corner and through the window she could see women sitting in chairs, gossiping, while their hair was tortured into Marcel waves, shingles, bobs and Eton crops. The smell of peroxide and hair lacquer wafted out through the doorway in gusts. She had never had her hair bobbed, but had chosen to wear it in a coil at the nape of her neck instead. She had never asked herself why. Today it felt so hot and heavy and uncomfortable, it would be a simple matter to step inside and ask the hairdresser to cut it all off. And yet she knew she wouldn't.

Another memory squirmed from the shadows and burst into her mind. It must have been an early one, for she was very young. She was perched on a stool before a mirror, her stockinged legs and little shoes swinging freely. Her little hands were folded carefully in her lap, because she'd been told not to touch any of the wonderful objects on the dressing table. The crystal stoppers and jars, the perfume and powder, the strange and fascinating pots of cosmetics.

She couldn't touch, but she could look – and she did, her brown eyes big with wonder.

This was a magic place!

There was someone standing behind her. While she gazed at the dressing table someone was brushing her hair. Long gentle strokes with a slight tug at the end, again and again, until her hair lay smooth as velvet against her back, a cloak of pale gold.

'Do not cut your hair, *ma petite,*' crooned a tender voice from the shadows behind her. 'So pretty, Evangeline. *Ma Petite Evangeline.*'

She peered into the mirror, trying to see who it was, but the shadows were too dense to see anything more than a shape. She was curious and unafraid, but the grown up Evie had learned that there was much to fear in her past, and she was frightened now.

Voices, images, feelings. They were all about her, far worse than they had been at any time in her life since she and her mother had run away ten years ago. Was this Daniel's doing? And the scheme they were involved in? How could she stop working for him when the money he was paying her would secure her family's future?

She realised suddenly that she was walking. She must have been moving for some minutes, because here she was about to turn into Earle Street. She had been so lost in her own thoughts that she hadn't taken in her surroundings. Another page missing, another paragraph blotted out.

There was a gangly youth lounging against a lamp post, probably the push's newest recruit. She ignored him, too caught up in her own concerns to care whether he snatched at her purse or called out something rude. In any event he did neither; just watched her while pretending not to.

Nearly home, Evie told herself, but the expected wave of relief didn't come. Instead she saw Gwen's house with a starkness that was even more depressing than usual. The place was so neglected. How much would it cost to have the roof fixed? The house needed painting, too, and the fence was missing several pickets. Still, what was the point of making repairs when they would be moving as soon as possible? Better to hold on to her money. Every penny counted.

'Evie?'

The voice startled her into turning. Vi Morgan stood on her doorstep, wriggling pudgy fingers at her. Evie put a polite smile on her face but shuddered inside. There was something creepy about the woman, as if you'd lifted up a stone and found a slug under it. She did not want to talk to Vi now.

'Did Gwen tell you I'd seen Billy in the tea leaves?'

'Yes, she did. It was very comforting, Mrs Morgan.' She kept walking. She was nearly past Vi's house.

'Did she tell you about Daniel and the French woman?'

Evie stopped. Her legs felt insubstantial, her body a weightless shell. It was an effort to turn.

'Frenchwoman?'

'That's it. Do you know her?' Mrs Morgan's face had assumed an even rounder appearance from curiosity, but there was no mistaking the trace of malice in her eyes. 'I saw it in the leaves. She's looking for you, Evie, and Daniel will help her to find you.'

Evie didn't know how she got home. She didn't hear Vi Morgan's, 'Well!' as she walked away. The Frenchwoman. The word rang in her head like a church bell with a dull bass sound. The sort of peal one heard at funerals or in times of crisis. The Frenchwoman and the blue went together. Everything was falling apart. Her tenuous hold on her world was giving way, like frayed string around a parcel. Soon the wrapping would burst open and the contents would spill out and scatter everywhere. If that happened Evie did not think she would ever be able to gather them back in.

Inside number 5 the air was cooler. Gwen was in the kitchen, scraping carrots. On the table a skinny plucked chicken was arranged in a baking dish, the carcass circled by a wreath of potatoes. Little Jimmy sat on the floor at her feet, hammering at pots with a wooden spoon. Evie bent and scooped him up, hugging him tightly. His warm little body was so precious, it seemed to help a bit, to pull her back from the brink of some catastrophe.

This was real. Jimmy and Gwen and ordinary life. The rest was in her mind and could be locked away. She had done it before; she could do it now.

'How was Dolly?' Gwen looked up. 'Couldn't she come back for a cuppa? What a shame.'

Reluctantly, Evie returned the struggling baby to the floor where he snatched up his treasures again. He had fair hair, like Evie, and dark eyes. She was always trying to see Billy in him, but it seemed as if the harder she tried the more his likeness eluded her.

'She has lots to do.' Evie answered at last, guiltier than ever about the lie. *Lies always come home to roost.* Someone had said that once. Perhaps it was her father. It sounded like something he would say, his mouth thin and straight, his bony face full of smug self-righteousness. *I don't want to hear another word from you, Evie. Not one more word.* She had spent her days being quiet, invisible – being afraid.

Gwen was nodding to show that she understood about Dolly, but there was concern in her eyes. 'You look done in, love. This heat! There'll be a storm soon. That'll clear the air – for a while, anyway.'

Evie sat down and looked at the chicken, trussed and stuffed and ready for the oven. Nausea curled deep in her stomach. 'I am a bit tired. Gwen, thank you for –'

'No need, love. I enjoy having the company of little Jimmy here. Good as Rudy Valentino any day!'

Evie laughed as Gwen had meant her to and some of the tension left her body. Hope bobbed to the surface. It would be all right. How did you see a Frenchwoman in a tea leaf, for God's sake? Vi Morgan had said those things to annoy her. Evie wouldn't believe otherwise; she wouldn't allow herself to.

Gwen was still peeling vegetables and Evie removed her yellow hat and placed it on the table. Shaking her hair free, she winced as her son played a particularly discordant note. In a moment she would go to her room upstairs and unfold the paper Daniel had given her and memorise the Beatson family secrets. Somehow tomorrow night she must do her job and play-act again. Pretend it was not all falling apart. Lock away all thoughts of the Frenchwoman and the blue nothingness and Daniel and the threats they all posed.

In their own very different ways.

CHAPTER 4

THE HOUSE, A LARGE TWO-STOREY box of a place, was in Camberwell, one of Melbourne's more affluent suburbs. Black clouds hid the stars when Daniel drove up the gravel drive. The air was thick with humidity and the threat of Gwen's storm, which had so far failed to arrive.

Evie was wearing a silver dress with a Turkish hem. Her hair was pinned under at the nape of her neck, the veil covering a face much paler than usual. Ignoring the flashes of warning she had been experiencing since yesterday she had worked herself into a state of unnatural calm. It would be all right, she told herself. She was just play-acting. She would have a few words with the Beatsons, a little pretend chat with their dead mother and then home to bed.

Nothing to it.

A shudder ran over her skin and with it came a sensation of pressure in her throat. She found it hard to take a breath. When Daniel clasped her hand she jumped and he gave her a look. 'Are you all right?' he murmured. He'd already rung the doorbell and there were footsteps approaching. *Too late to back out now.* Evie almost heard his thought in her own head.

'Of course.'

He looked wrung out. Shaven and dapper, yes, but somehow less than his usual confident self. Was there something wrong with him, too? She should ask him, she should force him to tell her the truth, but she was barely hanging on. Daniel's troubles would have to wait.

Miss Beatson opened the door. A tall, gaunt woman, she looked anxious. 'Oh, you're here!' she said. As the introductions were made her eyes skittered from Daniel to Evie and back again. 'Come in, then. Through here. My brother is waiting.'

'She expects us to turn into a pair of bats and fly around the house,' Daniel whispered as they followed her up the hallway.

Evie smiled and mouthed her words. 'We'll do that next time.'

She heard his soft laugh. The atmosphere seemed suddenly lighter, and she found she could breathe properly again.

The Beatsons were far older and more staid than their usual clients. Unlike Muriel Nelson's crowd, they weren't looking for distraction. They wanted results. Evie knew they were bound to be disappointed, but just how much was up to her.

The room the séance was to take place in was on the second floor. 'Mother's room,' Miss Beatson announced. A room from the Victorian era with heavy red curtains over the windows and fussy wallpaper, it was dense with the paraphernalia that had occupied the elderly Mrs Beatson's final years.

A host of small, bandy-legged tables was weighed down with porcelain figurines and Chinese vases and fussily framed photographs. A glass dome covering a long dead owl held pride of place on the marble mantelpiece.

'My mother was bedridden towards the end of her life,' Mr Beatson said. 'Everything she held dear was brought into this room so that she could be surrounded by the things she loved.'

A wooden lamp stand with a pink tasselled shade shone a dull light over the small sitting area by the fireplace. Four chairs were arranged in a rough circle. A tray with a cut glass decanter and four tiny glasses was placed on a side table, and Miss Beatson offered them sherry, her smile polite and nervous.

'I've dismissed the servants for the night,' she said. 'This is a private matter.'

Cannonades of thunder outside were muffled by the curtains. The electric light blinked off and on and they all stared at it, the Beatsons edgily, and Evie in the hope that it would go off. Séances were always better with a bit of atmosphere. But the light steadied and they were seated.

Slowly Evie lifted her veil and pretended not to notice that all eyes were upon her. She smiled faintly and nodded at Daniel. He leaned forward, serious and professional.

'We must all be very quiet,' he said soberly. 'Any disturbance could cause Miss Woodward to wake suddenly from her trance. Such a violent awakening could harm her.'

The Beatsons both nodded quickly. Evie hoped they would be as eager when the evening was over. She began to breathe deeply, relaxing her whole body and letting her head fall forward onto her chest. There was no sound, not even the ticking of a clock. The evening's performance had begun.

Daniel had taken her to a real séance once, so that she could make hers as authentic as possible. Since then Evie had held several séances of her own. It was easy, really, and she was a good mimic. People were so credulous. Sometimes she was ashamed of herself, all that moaning and gasping, all that acting. Billy wouldn't have liked it at all.

'Hello? Hello!'

The others jumped. Evie deepened her voice to give it an old woman's roughness. 'Is that you, Josephine? And Bernard, dear Bernard.'

'Mother?' Miss Beatson gave a little wriggle. 'Mother, is that you?'

'Yes, dear, it is I.'

'You sound in good form, Mother.'

'Better than she's been in years,' Bernard muttered.

'Well, and so I should be! I can walk again, my dears. Everyone can walk here.'

That gave them pause. Evie began to talk about the beauties around her, waxing lyrical and long. The Beatsons grew restless, but clearly they were not in the habit of interrupting their mother. At last Mr Beatson dared to ask the question they were desperate to have answered.

'Mother, please, you know how glad we are to hear from you. It's marvellous, isn't it, Josephine?'

Miss Beatson nodded violently.

'But, Mother, there's a problem. Your will.'

'My will?' The voice was so imperious the Beatsons stopped dead. 'Money is valueless here,

Bernard. I have no use for it. Perhaps you should prepare yourself for the hereafter.'

'I'll give that some thought, Mother, but in the meantime we need money to run the house, to look after the garden, to pay the servants. You wouldn't want your lovely house to fall into ruin.'

There was a pause. Evie lifted her head and looked from one to the other as if considering the question. 'I was a sick old woman,' she said at last in a querulous voice.

'Yes, Mother.'

'Now I am free of pain, I am young again in spirit. I am with your dear father.'

'You hated Father,' Bernard retorted and his eyes narrowed.

'All is love here,' Evie smiled again. Stirring and stretching she released a deep sigh.

'She's waking up,' Daniel murmured helpfully.

'But she can't!' Miss Beatson burst out. 'She hasn't told us where the will is. Mother, please, don't go!'

Thunder sounded outside, louder now, and the light flickered angrily. A shadow moved on the floor near the bed, stirring the coverlet. Green feline eyes gleamed through the tassel trimming. The air in the room felt so close and hot, and when the thunder rumbled again the vibration caused the beaded fringe on the lamp to shake.

The Beatsons glanced at each other uneasily.

Evie stirred again. "I'll come back and tell you where the will is, if you insist.' Her voice started to fade. 'Although how you can discuss money at a time like this is beyond me.'

'Mother, please —'

'I have so much to say to you both and you don't

want to listen.'

The thunder grumbled closer and the room shook again. Evie struggled to take a breath and felt a trickle of perspiration roll down her back. She longed to shuffle about in her chair. Her mouth was so dry that even one of the Beatsons' tiny glasses of sherry would have been welcome. But it was nearly over. Her patter had run its course. She had opened her mouth to finish it when a flash of movement caught her eye.

A cat leapt from the shadows by the bed. It was a large white cat with green eyes. It landed heavily on the arm of Evie's chair and bounded straight off again, upending the tray with the decanter and glasses. There was a terrible din.

Miss Beatson screamed hoarsely, clutching her brother's arm. Daniel had jumped up to save the decanter, too late. Evie opened her eyes wide just as thunder rolled again. And the lights went out.

Her eyes were open but blind in the darkness. She was in the cupboard under the stairs, where her father had locked her. Or was it somewhere else – a small space where she had crawled to hide? *Quiet, you must be very very quiet . . .* Wherever it was, she was suffocating, the black space pressing down on her. She tried to draw a breath and couldn't. She began to choke.

A loud and angry voice sounded beside her. It was Daniel, his accent slipping from the upper class English one he had assumed to something you'd catch in Earle Street. Evie didn't hear him. He struck a match and his face shone eerily out of the shadows. Behind him Miss Beatson's eyes were huge and gleaming in her white face. Evie didn't see her.

'Evie?' Daniel was shaking her arm. 'Evie, what is it?'

She stood up. 'Where am I?' she whispered. Her throat felt raw and made her voice sound harsh. It wasn't her voice. And even as she spoke again, Evie knew it wasn't in English.

'Please, where am I?'

'I beg your pardon?' Mr Beatson beside her peered anxiously into her face. He had a candle and the flame ducked and dived in his shaking hand. 'Miss Woodward, are you all right?'

Evie wasn't looking at him. She couldn't see him. She had realised where she was. It was a narrow tunnel, lit by lanterns hanging at intervals from the roof beams. Her hands brushed the rough surface of the wall and her shoes slipped on the damp ground. There was an intense feeling of fear. And there was someone following her, running her down as a hunter would his prey.

But I can still get away. If I can reach the opening at the bottom, if it is clear of rock and sand. The tide might be in, but I can swim. Like a fish. Not much further, not much further . . .

Hands closed about her neck. Strong and ruthless, fingers pressing down. She tried to scream, but couldn't. She tried to breathe, but couldn't. She was going to die here in this place and no one would help her and no one would find her and no one would ever know.

Miss Beatson screamed back while her brother shouted. Daniel leapt forward and grasped Evie by the arms. 'Evie,' he said between his teeth, 'for Christ's sake, snap out of it!'

'Je suis Genevieve. Pouvez-vous m'aider?'

'Stop it!' He shook her, hard.

'I am Genevieve,' Evie screamed, over and over again. 'I am Genevieve!'

That was when Daniel slapped her.

She had always had nightmares, ever since she was a child. They were another world, a dark night-time world that she only entered when she dared to sleep. She had learned to accept them, eventually. Her father had believed fear was an emotion that had to be mastered and he had taught her to master it by locking her in her room for hours on end and, when that didn't have the desired effect, in a cupboard in the kitchen. It was damp and dark and the sense of claustrophobia acute. A terrifying experience for a young child. No wonder she dreamed of small dark spaces.

The trick was to make the terror of the punishment greater than that of the nightmares. She woke screaming from dreams of being trapped in some small dark space, only to be locked in such a space to stop the dreams. It made no sense, but she had discovered that in her world the decisions of adults rarely did.

She learned not to sob hysterically but to pretend to be quiet and good. She learned not to bother Father. She learned to be as invisible as possible. She learned not to, as he would say, 'make a fuss'.

In other ways she was privileged. The family had money enough for her to go to a good day school

and to dress her well. Later, in Earle Street, she realised just how privileged her childhood had been
in that respect. She had never had to go without
shoes or a coat and her plate was always full of
food, her glass always filled with milk. In material
matters she was lucky.

At fourteen, she had begun to hear the Frenchwoman in her mind when she was awake, as well
as the voices of other people she had never met.
And she began to see the blue, that sheet of colour
that filled her mind and seemed to anticipate other
horrors. She puzzled over these matters endlessly,
but they were from no life she remembered or had
seen or read about. It was as if there was a whole
different world inside her, waiting to escape.

Evie knew it must never be allowed out. She had
learned by now that such surprises weren't well
received by her father. She kept her fantasies curled
up tight inside and remained the good and quiet
girl she had always tried to be. She had not been
locked in the downstairs cupboard for a long time
now, but the memory was strong. The sense of
being pressed into somewhere too small and where
it was hard to breathe did not often go away.

But no matter how hard she tried to be the good
and obedient daughter her father wanted, the
voices and the visions continued to afflict her. And
the nightmares grew worse, as if the make-believe
world inside her was feeding them. Night after
night they came, sometimes twice in the one night.
She had never been a bubbly and smiling child, but
now she grew so wan and silent that she might have
been a ghost. Teachers and neighbours noticed and
asked questions. And of course her father noticed.

'What is wrong with the girl?' he demanded.

Her mother turned frightened eyes in Evie's direction. 'She is of a certain age,' she said.

'Of a certain age? What is that supposed to mean?'

'She has strange fancies. It is not unknown for girls her age to have them.'

'What sort of strange fancies?' he asked impatiently.

Evie knew that in her own way her mother was trying to protect her. They were both victims, after all, but they were survivors, too. Sometimes it was necessary to bend the truth to protect oneself. And sometimes it was necessary to run away.

'I discourage her fancies, Frederick, as you have told me to discourage all oddities in her. I have brought her up to be the child you wanted. Quiet and occupied, polite and respectful.'

Her father grunted. He seemed to find the discussion distasteful and was glad to drop it. Her mother went back to her meal and silence reigned. There was a moment at bedtime when her father demanded to know whether she had any secrets and reminded her that all secrets were bad. 'I'll know if you're lying,' he had said.

Evie wondered if her father really could see into her mind and the idea was paralysing. Finally she was allowed to retire. But that night the nightmare came again, and it was worse than it had ever been before. She was glad to wake and when she opened her eyes, it was to find her father staring down at her.

She thought he was someone else. Another face was superimposed upon his, the face of a man she had never seen before, but who must never find her because he would hurt her. She didn't know how, but Evie knew that this man would lock her away under the earth and never let her out again. She started to scream and shake and hit at him with her fists. It was only when he caught her wrists and held her fast that she realised it was her father.

By the state of her bedclothes and her soaking nightgown, it was clear she had been calling out in her dream and woken him. There was a candle on the small table by the bed.

Breathing quickly they stared at each other. She was terrified and he – well, later she thought that he was frightened, too. The words came from a place she'd never known existed.

'*Qu'est-ce qui ne va pas, Papa?*' *What is the matter?*

He turned white. She still remembered his face hanging over her in the candlelight, the shocked blankness of it. He looked at her, not just as if she were a stranger – but as if she were *dangerous*.

'You're a bad girl, Evie. A wicked, lying girl.' His voice was shaking.

She thought he was going to strike her, but he didn't. He left her there. For the next week her mother looked more frightened than ever and she crept from room to room like a mouse. It was as if she knew something that Evie didn't, something too terrifying to speak of. A cloud hanging over them all was about to break.

Only it never did in the way Evie expected. Her father was late home – there was an important dinner at the place where he worked and they needed his help. Her mother was suddenly galvanised into action. They threw a few belongings into a suitcase and left. The front door swung open behind them and the light poured out onto the path. They ran all the way to the station and caught a train. And then another one. They didn't sleep, not even the next morning. And they kept running, until finally her mother reached a place she felt safe in.

And there they stayed. They changed their name and made up stories about themselves, pretending to be people they weren't. In a way it had been fun, but Evie had always sensed the seriousness behind the games.

She knew that her mother had never really been able to believe they had succeeded in escaping, not even when she died in 1925. Her last words had been a warning. 'Protect yourself, Evie. I have done my best for you, but you must always be careful.'

But how was she to be careful, Evie had often asked herself, when she did not know what the danger was? Or from which direction it would eventually come? Her mother had been afraid of her father and so had she when she was a child, but she was grown up now. He could not hurt her any more.

That had been her reasoning when she returned to Melbourne, and there had been a certain arrogance, too, when she had called herself by her proper name once more. Evangeline Woodward. It was almost a dare, like a cry into the dark night: *Come and get me . . .*

CHAPTER 5

E VIE WAS SHAKING SO BADLY she could hardly swallow the sherry. It stung her throat, made her cough and sent a wave of blessed warmth through her. Daniel kept one of her hands in his, as if he were afraid she might suddenly take another turn. She didn't blame him for his caution. He paid for her to perform, but this was well over the top. At least the Beatsons had forgotten all about their mother's will.

'I'm sorry,' she murmured. 'The cat. It was the cat. I mustn't be startled from my trance that way. It's bad, very bad.'

Black and white tiles in a long corridor. Running, her chest hurting. And then in front of her, the cat, its claws slipping on the marble, unable to find purchase. And always behind her, the man she couldn't see . . .

Miss Beatson looked uneasy, twisting her fingers around an embroidered scrap of a handkerchief. 'It was Mother's cat,' she explained stiffly. 'I suppose it wanted to talk to her, too.'

Evie swallowed and managed a smile. 'Did you find out what you wanted to know?' she asked blithely.

The Beatsons exchanged a glance. 'Oh yes,' they said politely. They looked sick. Evie had the satisfaction of knowing they believed in her even if they never wanted her in their house again.

Outside, Daniel opened the passenger door of the car and helped her in. She slumped in her seat, with her neck arched and head back. She needed to breathe. The sensation of suffocation was still strong. She expected him to demand answers but he said nothing and drove her home in silence. Lightning flashed across the sky at lengthening intervals as the storm moved off. Then rain began to fall, soft and persistent, and Evie wound her window down a crack and savoured the cool, fresh air.

At Earle Street, Daniel stopped the car, lit a cigarette and waited.

'It was . . . the Frenchwoman,' she said, and her voice was husky from screaming. 'She was looking for me, Vi Morgan said so, and that you'd help her find me. You have, Daniel. I ran away once and left her behind, but somehow all that we've been doing has set her onto me again. She's found me.'

He turned and eyed her warily. 'What Frenchwoman? What are you talking about?'

She knew she had to stop now, offer some excuse and make him laugh. And yet she heard her own voice saying, 'You remember, Daniel. You know what I'm talking about.'

'Tell me, Evie!' He was angry now. 'If you're going to go around spewing French, I need to understand why. Tell me!'

'*Qu'est-ce qui ne va pas, monsieur?*' she whispered. *What's the matter?* 'Do you remember now?'

His eyes showed that he did, and he watched her

through the cigarette smoke. 'What's that got to do with now? I remember that night at the Grande, of course I do. I remember you saying that. So what?'

So what? She sighed. That night at the Grande. She remembered that night as if it had only just happened. She had been lying on the ground outside the Grande Ballroom with her face bruised and scratched and her lip bleeding. There was a row of windows in the wall above her and the shadows within swayed and twirled as the dancers passed by. No one knew she was there.

And then Daniel had come. He looked down at her and reached out to feel for the pulse in her neck. She was dizzy and confused and didn't know where she was. His mouth was a grim line, although later she realised that his anger was not for her, but for the man who had done this.

'*Qu'est-ce qui ne va pas, monsieur?*' she'd breathed.

He'd laid his hand gently on her shoulder. 'Do you speak English?' he'd ventured. '*Parlez-vous anglais?*' he'd tried, using a line he'd picked up somewhere.

She blinked back at him. His words made no sense at first, and then with a jolt they did. Despite the pain in her head she sat up. 'What do you mean?' she demanded hysterically. 'Of course I speak English!'

She had been frightened. It was the first time she had spoken French since that night when she was fourteen, before she and her mother had run away. She had always blamed the Frenchwoman for their desperate flight.

Daniel had taken her back to his office, a small box of a room downstairs off the stage in the

Grande. She was wearing a simple white shift, short and with beadwork about the neckline and hem. She'd made it herself on a friend's sewing machine. Her shoes were narrow and high and cut into her feet, giving her a blister on one heel. She'd lost one of her shoes, anyway, and her bag, beaded like the dress. Her makeup was smeared, the lipstick all around her mouth and the kohled eyes like bruises on her pale skin. One of the scratches ran across her left cheek, and there was a cut on her lip where the man had hit her when she wouldn't cooperate.

She'd told Daniel that she didn't know why she'd trusted that man. Something about his smile. He'd seemed nice, and she was lonely. A breath of air, he'd said, and before she knew it he had led her around the side of the building, away from the crowd. Pressing hard against her he'd tried to kiss her and she'd known then that she had to fight him. So she had hit and kicked him, until he'd grown tired of her resistance and knocked her down. The fight had gone out of her then.

He'd begun to unbutton his trousers and she'd tried to scream, but there had been no air left in her lungs. That was when Daniel had come to her rescue. Her hero. He'd grabbed hold of the man and punched him twice, once in the face and once in the stomach. The man had doubled over, retching, but Daniel had ignored him after that and attended to her.

He had sat her down in a worn leather chair and filled a bowl with water from the tap in the corner. He'd used a handkerchief to bathe her cuts and scratches, holding the cool cloth against her lip to reduce the swelling. His hands were so tender, his handsome face so intent. She felt tears hot in her eyes and was powerless to stop them slipping down her cheeks. At one time she had lived every minute of every day with the fear of being punished and hurt, and even when she and her mother had run away, they had still been afraid. But lately the fear had left her. She had her job at the tea rooms and her friends, and she had felt safe for the first time in many years.

And now this, as if to remind her that she was only fooling herself.

Above them, on the stage, the band played a fast number and the dancers shook the Grande with their youthful enthusiasm. It all seemed a long way away from Evie and Daniel.

'I've been watching you dance,' he said, as if she wasn't sitting there, crying with no sound, and he wasn't cleaning up the damage another man had done to her. 'You came in with a girl. Dark hair bobbed, yellow dress cut low. I saw you with that bastard. I wanted to warn you then that I didn't think you should be here, a girl like you. You're too good for this place.'

She met his eyes. They were dark and acute – the sort of eyes that saw right through you and out the other side. She liked his voice, too, and wanted him to go on speaking.

'That bastard's done this before. I've warned him. I'll see to him, don't worry. He won't be back.'

She believed him. The danger and violence in his words were convincing. He'd avenge her and she was glad.

He turned her face to one side and then the other, his gaze wandering over her high cheekbones, the long straight nose and big, dark eyes. Her hair was the colour of wheat and it was long. It was falling free of the coil at the nape of her neck, wisps sticking to her damp skin. He brushed her lip with his thumb and frowned at the swelling.

'Are you all right now?' he'd asked.

She'd nodded. There was something about this man that reminded her of herself – she sensed a soul as adrift as her own, and that was frightening, but also exciting. She could fall deep with this man into the dark emptiness that she had always avoided. She could lose herself, or find herself, if she were brave enough.

He leaned forward. 'Where are you living?'

'I'm staying with the friend you saw, the one in the yellow dress. I work at the Peking Tea Rooms.'

He frowned. 'You don't sound like a girl who serves tea. You sound like a lady in a flower shop.'

She laughed, but it sounded close to breaking and she covered her mouth with her hand. 'Thank you,' she said in a voice muffled by her fingers. 'I think.'

He was watching her keenly, as if he was trying to read her mind.

She slipped her hand into his and squeezed it gently. 'Thank you,' she said again.

He told her that he worked at the Grande Ballroom. She stayed downstairs in the little room and after everyone had gone and the ballroom was empty, he took her back upstairs and they had danced to the music in their heads. He had held her close, his chin on the crown of her head and his body pressed to hers.

It had been a magical night – one she had never

forgotten.

Even when he had bent down and kissed her, making her lip sting again, she hadn't wanted to stop him. But he hadn't done more than kiss. He'd taken her home to the terrace house in Richmond which she shared with her friend. He'd told her to be more careful, and that he would call back and see if she was all right.

She had gone to bed, feeling as if she had found the man of her dreams.

But the next morning her bruises ached, her head was pounding and the magic had given way to doubt and fear. When he called to check on her, she could see that he was a man who would never be able to give her the safety and security she craved. Oh, he was a kind man, a nice man – but not *the* man for her. Evie didn't trust easily, and she had no intention of trusting Daniel.

Still, they became friends. He came to see her at the Peking Tea Rooms, and flirted with the other girls. He never singled any particular one out, and she knew she was the one he had come to see, but still, she had no intention of falling in love with him. In turn she entered into his shadowy world. He introduced her to his friends or the men he worked for. Gunner Connor was the worst, but she could see at a glance that they were all of a similar type. Liars and cheats, they broke the law when they could and didn't think twice about hurting someone who crossed them. They took risks, lived in the shadows and were forever looking over their shoulders rather than forward to the future.

Evie never looked back, if she could help it.

But that was Daniel's life, and she could not see

it changing. They were both survivors, yes, but for her to survive she had to feel safe. And Daniel wasn't safe at all.

Then one Sunday he took her to lunch at Earle Street, at Gwen's and Billy's. And that was the end of it – and the beginning.

'So what?' he said now. She looked up into that familiar handsome face and forced a laugh.

She still couldn't tell him. She wanted to, but she was still afraid, even after all these years. She still could not trust him or herself – couldn't take the risk. She could not say, *I thought I was cured, Daniel. I thought I had left the Frenchwoman behind me, but now she's found me again. I don't think I can work for you any more; it's not safe. She's getting stronger and I am getting weaker. Who knows what will happen next?*

But she didn't say any of it out loud.

'Evie,' he said, 'I don't know what's going on here. If you won't tell me, I can't make you. You always had your secrets and I've never asked you for anything before, have I?'

His dark eyes challenged her and she shook her head.

'Well, I am now. This time I need you.'

The words shocked her with their raw simplicity. Daniel needed her?·

He laughed when he saw the look on her face, but there was a tautness in his body and an urgency in his voice that was new. 'Yes, that's right. I need you. You're good at this. You have the face, the voice, the manners. You can make people believe anything.'

'I can't. I'm so sorry, but I can't.'

'Evie, I need you to come to Blue Waters with

me. I need that job.'

'Why?' she cried. 'You said before that it didn't matter. Now you say it does. Why that particular job, Daniel?'

He lit another cigarette and stared at the rising smoke. 'You remember that bloke you saw the other day, when you came up to the office?'

'With the Gladstone bag?' She pushed a strand of hair back behind her ear and found that her hand was shaking. 'I remember. I couldn't think who it was, but I knew his face. He was one of Gunner Connor's chaps, wasn't he?'

Gunner Connor had been a bit like Daniel once, a schemer who was always looking to make some easy money. But unlike Daniel he'd grown. He'd swallowed up the smaller mobs, taking over legal and illegal businesses with or without their owners' consent. Now Connor's tentacles reached onto every street corner and into every laneway. And he had a reputation for violence and greed that was unparallelled in the Melbourne underworld.

'I owe Connor money, Evie, and I've got to repay it. You know what he's like.'

'Money for what?'

'The agency. To get it started.'

She shook her head, trying to deny what she knew he was asking.

'The Grieves job will make me enough to clear my debt.'

'Surely Connor will give you more time? I thought he was a friend of yours.'

He smiled at her, but the look in his eyes was bleak. 'Sure. I used to be a friend of his, so he won't kill me straightaway. He'll just break a bone or two and play with my face. And if I still don't pay him, *then* he'll kill me.'

She felt weak and giddy. She wanted to tell him that he was a fool and should never have got himself in so deep, but she had never told him what to do. That part of his life was private. Only Billy had been allowed to offer advice like that.

'I'm not a good bet at the moment,' she warned him. 'You need someone who won't let you down and right now – I can't promise I won't.'

He reached across and pressed his finger to her lips. 'You've never let me down, *I*'ve let *you* down. This time, I thought – I hoped it would be different. I wanted to help you and make it better for you. I wanted that more than anything.' His face was close, his eyes dark and shadowed.

'You have helped me, Daniel,' she whispered, pushing away his hand.

He shook his head. 'Yeah,' he muttered. 'Helped you so much that you've just had a fit of hysterics over a cat.'

'It's difficult.'

He glanced at her sideways and then shrugged, seeing that she had no intention of taking him into her confidence. 'Look, I don't expect you to trust me. But I'll never let anyone hurt you, never. I promise I'll keep you safe. Help me pay off Connor and I won't ask you for anything again. I'll get right out of your life, if that's what you want. Evie?'

He was desperate. He had to be. He had never begged before, or asked her to do something that he could see was tearing her in two. Even at his most confident, he always kept a back door or two open, so that he could make his escape. Why was this time different?

'There's something you're not telling me, isn't there? We've been earning so much. How can you still owe him? There's more to it, isn't there?'

He gave a humourless laugh. 'Is there?'

'I need to know. I won't make a decision until I know.'

'You won't like it, Evie.'

'I still need to hear it. The truth, Daniel. Can you manage that?'

'I can manage it, all right,' he retorted. 'Probably better than you can. When have you ever told anyone the truth? Who is this Frenchwoman?' But he didn't wait for her excuses; he knew her too well. 'How about tomorrow I take you and Jimmy for a drive in the country? A day off. Will you come? We can talk as much as you like.'

A drive in the country? Perhaps he expected her to refuse, but she had no intention of doing so. If Daniel really needed her help then he would tell her the truth, and then – then it would be up to her. 'Tomorrow? All right.'

'Tomorrow then,' he said, but he didn't seem happy about it.

She climbed out of the car and walked towards number 5. She glanced back as she reached the corner, but he was still there. She knew he wouldn't go until she was safely inside the house.

He never did.

That fact alone should have scared the life out of her, but instead it gave her a dangerously warm glow. Daniel cared. Perhaps she just hadn't realised how much until now.

The hot summer had turned the grass brown and the trees drooped in the paddocks, their leafy hems trimmed by resting sheep or cattle. A solitary horse stood, its tail swishing at flies.

Daniel's Oldsmobile hummed along past fences and farmhouses and Evie pointed out anything she thought might amuse her son. The day was warm and he wore a sailor suit and a bonnet. The breeze had turned his plump cheeks pink.

It was the first time Evie had been out with Jimmy for ages. When he was very little, Billy had taken them several times to the beach at St Kilda where they found their own little patch of sand among the hundreds of other Melbourne families. Sometimes a band had played in the rotunda, and tea and other refreshments could be had for a reasonable price, if one didn't bother to bring one's own.

Today Evie had packed them a basket – left-over chicken sandwiches, ginger beer and a slab of sultana cake. Gwen thought she was going out with Dolly and Dolly's boyfriend.

'Don't let little Jimmy get sunburned now,' she had reminded her. If she was disappointed not to have been asked, or not to have met the elusive Dolly, she hid it well. Evie suspected it was because she was glad of some time on her own for once.

Evie had met Daniel at the office and he'd driven them from there. She felt awkward and wondered whether he did too. Last night had been unpleasant and the subsequent conversation unsettling.

Although Evie had slept well, her dreams had been strange and dark, and she still felt tired. The Beatson séance was not something she wanted to repeat. It had been a warning she would be a fool to ignore.

Then what was she doing here, letting Daniel persuade her to do just that?

The country road was narrow and quiet. Despite herself, Evie felt it taking her far away from all her problems. She wondered if Daniel would like to keep driving, just keep going, and not go back. They could leave everything behind them.

Billy, too? When she thought of Billy now, it was usually as he had been at number 5 Earle Street. Like a faded, much handled photograph, he sat at the head of the table tucking into Gwen's hearty meals, or he smiled at her from the front door as he left for his job every morning, or he held her in his arms in their bed at night. What would happen when she finally moved away to some other address? Would the memories of Billy be left behind? Would he be forgotten all the sooner?

'Evie?'

She glanced across at Daniel, glad to be distracted. 'What?'

'Are you hungry yet?'

'A bit. Jimmy could do with a walk.' The little boy was shifting about on her lap.

Daniel smiled and reached across to ruffle his hair. 'Hang on, mate. There's a place up ahead. I used to come here when my dad was alive,' he explained. 'He was brought up around here. He always said he was a country boy at heart and proud of it.'

Daniel rarely spoke about his past. Evie knew he had been in trouble with the police when he was young, but Billy had always said that was because when his father died, his mother had spent all her time grieving for the man rather than caring for the boy.

'This is it.' They turned down a track and drove a short distance. A big, gnarled red gum, its branches twisted into grotesque curls and turns, held court over a sparsely grassed corner of an empty field.

Daniel parked his car and they laid out a blanket and the food. Jimmy trotted about, exploring his tiny kingdom. Evie handed Daniel a sandwich and he poured her a ginger beer. The drink fizzed up her nose and made her eyes water.

'She still makes it then?' Daniel grinned wryly, holding up the bottle of honey coloured liquid.

She nodded and found her voice. 'In the laundry. Bottles explode regularly.'

Little Jimmy sat down hard on his well-pad-ded bottom and looked so surprised that they both laughed. Daniel's eyes were warm and dark, intimate. Evie looked away and pretended not to notice.

The air was very still. The heat captured the scent of eucalyptus, adding to the smells of dust and gin-ger beer and chicken. They mostly ate in silence, lulled by the warmth. Daniel stretched out on his back, arms folded under his head and tipped his hat over his eyes. He lay perfectly still with polished shoes crossed. He was like a fashionable adver-tisement for men's clothing. He had always been the sort of man that women looked at twice, Evie reminded herself as she watched him from the cor-ner of her eye.

And there had been women – lots of them –

before and after she had known him. No one special, though; no one he seemed to want to hold on to. Billy always said that Daniel was a romantic. She hadn't thought of him like that, but she remembered the night at the Grande and the way they had danced, all alone, in the big empty space and suddenly she knew it was true. He wanted a woman he could love with his mind, body and soul and he wouldn't be satisfied with less.

The baby tugged drowsily at his bottle with his eyes half closed and his plump fingers gradually loosening their grip. As Evie watched him, she loved him so much it was like pain. He was lucky, she knew that, a lucky little boy. Her own childhood had been a barren desert by comparison.

'Evie?'

Daniel was holding out the ginger beer bottle. She shook her head, and he poured the rest of it into his own glass. Small black ants wandered across the blanket seeking crumbs. Evie watched them and kept them away from her sleeping son's soft, vulnerable flesh, at the same time admiring their determination as they clambered over small mountains and climbed out of deep valleys in the well-worn wool.

Daniel's shirt sleeves were rolled up above his elbows, and dappled sunlight caught the dark hairs on his arms and the backs of his capable hands. He wore a thick gold signet ring on one finger. Evie watched him surreptitiously as he removed his hat and leaned back, gazing up through the thickened network of branches. He narrowed his eyes and his mouth turned straight and grim. Whatever he was thinking didn't seem to please him very much.

'You'd better tell me now,' she said quietly. 'Before Jimmy wakes up.'

He turned his head and looked at her. Evie waited, pretending not to be taken aback by the sudden watchful tension in his dark eyes.

'I owe money,' he said bluntly. 'You're right, I did borrow to set up the agency, but I didn't borrow it from Connor. And again you're right, I have paid all that back. But there's something else – another loan.' He shrugged, as if the details were unimportant. 'Connor didn't like it when I didn't ask him for the money. He enjoys it when I'm indebted to him – not just with money but with favours, too. He needs to believe he's my boss; it makes him feel good about himself.'

'I'm sure it does.' Connor was jealous of Daniel, Evie had sensed it the first time she saw them together. He was good at the grubby stuff, but he would never be a Daniel Roxburgh and he knew it. Perhaps that was why he resented Daniel so much and wanted to bring him down. It had become an obsession.

'When he found out about my loan, he said his feelings were hurt. He paid it off for me and took it over. So now I owe him, instead. But if we take the Grieves job, then I'll be able to slip his leash once and for all. I'll be free of him, Evie.'

And if you don't? she thought.

'I don't understand,' she said. 'What is this other loan?' It occurred to her suddenly that Daniel, apart from paying her, hadn't had much spare change recently. His office in Little Lonsdale Street was seedy and he was sleeping there, living there. What had happened to his house? And he'd seemed worried. For Daniel to be worried it had to be serious indeed. Where was the money going? They were making lots with the agency, so it had to be going somewhere.

Obviously it was something he hadn't wanted her to know about.

'Are you working for the police?' she asked abruptly.

He laughed. 'Why do you ask that?' he bluffed. 'I see them off and on; we use each other. That's what it's like. Most of the time I don't think there's much difference between them and Connor.' He picked up his hat and turned it in his hands, fiddling with the brim. 'There's a new detective. Molloy. I don't know what to make of him. Maybe you saw him the other day. He's pushing me to help him get Connor; he wants me to give evidence, but I'd have to be an idiot, wouldn't I, to agree to that?'

'Dangerous,' she murmured.

'For me, yeah.'

Was he tempted? Connor in jail would mean Daniel was free of the other man, but if Connor found out who put him there . . .

'You haven't told me what this other loan is about.'

'Believe me, you don't want to hear.' Daniel tossed his hat down. 'I can handle this. All I need to know is whether you'll do the Grieves job with me.'

'Have you been paying me too much? Is that it? I can give you some back if you need it.' It would mean she couldn't move out of Earle Street as soon as she would like, but that couldn't be helped. She really didn't want Daniel with a broken nose, or worse. *Gunner* Connor hadn't acquired his nick-name without reason.

'No,' he groaned, 'I don't want your money. You've earned every penny. It isn't that.'

'Then what? For God's sake, what is it? Why can't you tell me?'

He was looking at her so helplessly. Daniel, who was never without a witty reply or a counter plan. Billy once said that no one and nothing could stop Daniel; that he'd live forever. Maybe Billy had been wrong. A sense of dread crept over her.

'Daniel? You're frightening me, and I don't like it.'

'You'll hate me if I tell you,' he said quietly.

'Why would I hate you?' she demanded, her voice breaking. 'I know what you did to the man who hurt me the night we met. Did you think I didn't know that? I know what happened to him. I won't hate you; I couldn't ever hate you.'

He'd seen in her face that it was the truth, that whatever was between them was stronger than any secret he was keeping from her. She knew the moment he gave in and for a brief time she was relieved. Until he began to speak.

'It's Billy.'

'Billy?'

'That lunchtime I met him at the factory, the day he died. He told me he owed money to the bookmakers. Lots of it. He bet on the horses, did it all the time, always had done as long as I knew him. Gwen didn't know and he didn't want her to – and then you. You thought the world of him. He couldn't tell you, he said, not when things were such a struggle. He couldn't bear to see the look in your eyes. He asked me to help him because I knew the people involved. So I took the debts on. I'm not saying it was easy, with that and the agency, but it was all right. I could manage it. And then Connor found out about Billy's horseracing debts and took them over. He's been looking for a way to get a hold on me – he thinks I'm doing too well without his help. He was smiling when he told me that he wanted the money paid off within the month. Said if I didn't do it then he'd come around to number 5 and sort it out himself. I'm sorry, Evie. This wasn't meant to happen. I hoped I'd never have to tell you, I really did. For your sake, and for Billy's.'

She didn't know what to say. Billy, spending his hard-earned money on the horses? Billy, in debt and too frightened to tell her? Billy begging Daniel to help him and then going back to work and –

'Daniel,' she whispered. 'No, you don't think he –'

'No!' He laughed angrily. 'No, he didn't do himself in. Never. It was an accident. Don't you go thinking that! Billy wouldn't have left you if he could have helped it. You were the world to him.'

And of course he was right. Billy wouldn't have left her alone. She felt relief, and a strange shaky sensation that was shock. Billy Rose, her beloved and perfect husband, had not been perfect at all.

'I can never tell Gwen,' she managed. 'She'd be devastated.'

'Then don't tell her.' He sighed. 'I'm sorry. Connor's doing this to get at me and now you've got dragged into it.'

'No, no, there's nothing to be sorry about. I – it's a shock.'

'Don't think any less of Billy,' he said gently. 'He was a man, not a saint. But he was a good man.'

'I wish you'd told me sooner.' Shock gave way to anger as she remembered his recent haggard looks. 'You should have said!'

'What was the point? You couldn't afford to pay back that money and I could. Did you want them coming around to number 5, taking away whatever was worth anything?'

For a moment she saw it in her mind – Connor and his men carrying Gwen's wireless away and Gwen begging them to let her listen to Peter Dawson one last time.

'No, I didn't want that,' she whispered.

He breathed a sigh of relief. 'It was the only way, Evie. Believe me. I did it for Billy.'

She looked at him and then turned away. He was the same and he hadn't changed. He wasn't an angel and although he had done an honourable thing, she still didn't know whether she could trust him or not. What he had just told her was the truth, she decided. He looked so anguished at the knowledge that he had had to sully her memory of Billy, the Billy he was still protecting, just as he was protecting her and Jimmy and Gwen. It had to be the truth.

He was speaking again in that serious voice. 'Evie, I promise you that after Blue Waters I can stop – *we* can stop. For good.'

'Daniel –'

'But you see that if we stop now, Connor will still want his money. He'll come and get me and then he'll come around to number 5. You don't want that, believe me.'

Evie took a breath. He was right; she didn't.

The lines deepened around his eyes and his smile was grim. 'Trust me,' he said.

She laughed. 'Do I have a choice?' Already she felt as if she was balanced precariously on a narrow ledge and it would be so easy to fall off. Could she risk it? Could she risk another encounter with the Frenchwoman? 'You promise this is our last job?' she said quietly.

He tried not to look triumphant. 'This is the last one, I promise.'

'Then I agree.'

'Thank you.'

She avoided his hand and began to pack the food back into the basket, ants and all. What could she say? That she was terrified of what would happen to her now that the Frenchwoman had found her. The nightmare was starting all over again and she was trapped into doing the very thing that seemed to be making the nightmare stronger. She knew that she could not run away this time. She had a child, she had Gwen, and they wouldn't survive it.

'It'll be all right,' he said.

'Of course it will,' she agreed, but she didn't mean it.

Things were as far from all right as they could possibly be.

CHAPTER 6

E VIE SHADED HER EYES AS they left the inner city behind them and headed around the bay. The late afternoon sun turned the land a glowing gold and stretched out the shadows, while the water was flat and gleaming like glass.

Leo Grieves had sent a note. He would expect them at Blue Waters before dark. His mother would be there; she had travelled from her permanent home in the Western District. His brother and wife would also be there, as well as several guests. It would be the perfect weekend party.

The Grieves family was powerful. Evie had learned a little more about them since hearing Daniel's brief summary. The old man, Sir Henry, had made his money from gold before retiring to one of the more exclusive bayside areas to build an appropriate edifice. Raymond had been the son of his first wife and Leo the son of his second. Both had distinguished themselves in their own right: Leo in the army and Raymond in the world of moving pictures.

Leo had dabbled in politics since the war and was

now reputed to be writing a novel. Raymond had made a moderately successful film and was about to make another. They were wealthy, handsome and fashionable.

'Have you seen Blue Waters before?' Daniel's voice broke the long silence. They had hardly spoken a word since they left his office. Evie was quiet because she was worried about what might happen and she imagined Daniel felt the same.

Their last case, and their most important one. So much depended on the outcome.

And she was angry with him. He had been almost right when he said if he told her the truth she would hate him. She didn't hate him, but she found herself close to it. How dare he keep Billy's debts from her? How dare he play the martyr like that? If she had known, she could have helped. Instead she felt foolish and helpless – a victim of circumstance – and she had sworn never to feel that way again.

'Evie?'

'No, I haven't,' she snapped.

He glanced at her. 'A tasteless pile of brick and stone.'

'I can't wait.'

'You don't have to. There it is.'

'Good God,' she whispered.

It reared up on the cliff before them. A tower rose from one corner, windows gleamed in the sun, giving the impression of a fairytale castle.

'But Daniel, it's beautiful!' she cried, forgetting her animosity.

A road wound towards it, with a number of houses dug into the hillside on either side. A new housing development was going up at a brisk rate, and perhaps, one day, Blue Waters itself would be demolished to make way for more little boxes. But for now the Grieves edifice loomed over all else.

The road ahead was flanked by white stone pillars, the intricately decorated wrought iron gate standing open. A few overgrown shrubs lined the driveway, and through them Evie caught tantalising glimpses of the house. And then abruptly the road opened out onto a wide forecourt and the house seemed to jump out at her. The exclamation of pleasure she had been about to make died on her lips.

What had seemed eye–catching and exotic from a distance was oddly jarring at close-quarters. The proportions were wrong. The tower seemed squat rather than soaring and the rest of the house was heavy – all straight lines rather than curves. It looked like a stately home that had been designed by a prison architect.

As her gaze slid over the solid stone facade there was a tiny stab of pain, as if from sharp glass, between her eyes. Sudden – and gone again as quickly.

He was speaking but she didn't really hear him. He was saying something about self-aggrandisement and people with more money than sense. He would have spent the money on fast cars and expensive suits, she supposed. Or maybe not. Maybe Daniel secretly longed for a monstrosity just like this.

He had parked the car. A statue of Cupid, mottled with age and damp, peered at them through the salt-speckled leaves. Evie stepped carefully out of the car. She was wearing a coffee-coloured, knee-length dress with four tiers of soft pleats below the waist. She'd worn it before, but the shoes were new, cream leather with pointed toes and Louis heels. Gwen had said she looked fit for the best company and there had been a glint of pride in her eyes which made Evie feel twice as guilty.

This was the last time. She was tired of lying and tired of being afraid. After this weekend, Billy's debts would be cleared and she and Daniel could go their separate ways. It would be a relief, in a way, never to have to see him again.

Never to have to be reminded of what Billy had done.

The sun had dipped further, its rays spearing past the shadows, illuminating Blue Waters like the spotlights in one of Raymond Grieves's pictures. The neglect was now more apparent. Perhaps not even the sort of money the Grieves family had was enough to keep a house like this in good order.

Daniel had collected their luggage. The main entrance was at the top of a shallow flight of stairs, flanked by stone lions. The front door was of heavy dark wood with stained glass panels on either side. The bell rang sharply when he pulled it.

'I won't need to pretend,' Evie said. 'This place has to be genuinely full of spooks.'

Daniel frowned. He clearly wasn't in the mood for levity. 'Just do what we agreed and everything will be all right.'

'Of course.' She widened her eyes at him in mock innocence.

His frown deepened and then miraculously transformed into a smile as the door opened. A woman, young and bright, gestured them in with a smile. 'I'm Honora Stubbs, the housekeeper. Mr Roxburgh, is it? And Miss Woodward? Please, do come in.'

Inside the entrance hall was long and rather bare, apart from a large gilt-framed mirror that hung above a black marble fireplace. Once the hall must have been full of Victorian clutter – ferns and marble and *objets d'art*.

There was a thump overhead, but before Evie could do more than glance up, Honora had led them towards a sitting room with faded chintz curtains and a bowl of fresh roses on the table.

'Mrs Grieves wanted a word with you both before you settle into your rooms,' she said with quiet efficiency. 'I'll just tell her you're here.'

Evie wandered about the room, touching the gold and ormolu clock on the mantelpiece, inspecting an oil painting of a very clean shepherd with his very clean sheep. The carpet was old but beautiful, full of strange Eastern flowers and beasties.

'Let me do the talking,' Daniel said. He was leaning against the window sill. 'You just be enigmatic.'

'When should I begin my performance?'

They'd worked on their plan of action. Cool, distant and businesslike, Daniel had led her through her part. 'I'll leave that to you. But build up to it. Always keep a bit back. Draw them in.'

The door opened. 'Mr Roxburgh and Miss Woodward, I've been so looking forward to meeting you both!'

At seventy she was well-preserved and her pale blue eyes were sharply intelligent. As Daniel moved to take Leila Grieves's hand she glanced past him to Evie, just briefly, but Evie felt the impact of her inspection. For a moment it seemed to sear her, look inside and hold her.

Evie felt her brittle tranquillity shiver. A voice spoke in her head, clear and precise and absolutely terrifying.

You're a proper little lady, aren't you?

Daniel watched her with a frown. Evie shook herself, gathering her wits, as Leila cast a glance over Daniel. From his brown and grey pin-striped suit, to his recently trimmed dark hair and his air of complete confidence. Evie had always enjoyed seeing how other people viewed him and watching him deceive them with whatever part he was playing. Now she thought of the secret he had kept from her and knew that she had been taken in, too. That wasn't fun.

But Leila Grieves evidently liked what she saw. She smiled, the corners of her mouth turned up flirtatiously as if she were a fraction of her age.

Evie found it difficult to believe that she had been a lowly servant when Sir Henry Grieves married her in 1880. The long silk dress in a medley of colours was elegant, and her figure, famous when she was young, was perhaps a little fuller but it was still striking. Her fair hair had faded to white and was twisted into an elegant chignon – and then there was the jewellery: heavy rings on her slim fingers, a sparkling diamond pendant about her gently sagging throat and an emerald pinned to her dress above her breast.

This was not a woman who could ever be ignored.

Daniel had told Evie a story about her meeting with Sir Henry. Evidently Leila had been a servant at Blue Waters a full year when he finally proposed to her. She had held out that was the thing. Whereas those before her had given in, dazzled by Henry's wealth and power, she had said no. And it had driven him mad. Mad enough to go down on his knees one day on the upper landing, where she was dusting the furniture, and put a ring on her finger.

'Ah, Miss Woodward, of course.' Once again Evie met the pale eyes and felt their power. 'When Leo told me about Muriel's little cocktail party, I knew I must have you both come to Blue Waters. My own dear Penelope, another seeker after the spiritual truth, has told me a little about the house and the souls it contains, but I will be very interested to know what you see during your stay here.' The smile hardened slightly. 'Do you know Penelope Poindexter, Miss Woodward? She is quite famous in some circles.'

Evie freed her hand. 'No, I haven't met her, although I know her by reputation, of course.'

Leila Grieves's pale eyes summed her up, or attempted to. Evie reminded herself that her hostess would judge her by her voice, her manners, the well-bred air that she had been taught as a child. She could not know the truth – no one could.

'My husband Henry built the house. He was an ordinary man with extraordinary abilities. The gold rush had begun when he arrived in Victoria and that was how he made his fortune. He was a millionaire.' She gave Daniel another of her flirtatious smiles. 'Mr Roxburgh, you'll have to ask Leo about Henry – he knows the story much better than I. He's writing his father's biography.'

'Do you reside in the house, Mrs Grieves?' Daniel asked. 'It's just that your son said you were living in the western district.'

Leila Grieves nodded, a hint of sadness in her smile. 'I'm afraid so. Blue Waters is far too big for us now. Raymond says it would make a wonderful movie set for a medieval romance, perhaps, with sword fights on the staircase and maidens calling for help from the rooftop.' She laughed, to show she was joking. 'The house is beyond us, I am afraid. It will have to be sold, and soon. The land is very valuable. More and more people want to live by the bay. This may well be the last time we are all here together like this, Mr Roxburgh, so you should think yourself privileged to be a part of this weekend gathering.'

Daniel made the appropriate sounds.

'Now —' She rose neatly and easily to her feet. 'You must go up to your rooms and settle in. Dinner will be in an hour. We dress, of course. Leo will be here and you may be acquainted with some of my other guests. I believe you are the very height of fashion at the moment, Mr Roxburgh.'

She pulled a dark green cord by the door and Evie heard a far away peal.

'I am sorry you could not discover where old Mrs Beatson hid her will, Miss Woodward.'

Her pale eyes looked innocent, but Evie wasn't deceived. The elderly woman was indulging herself with a little bit of malice.

'I was sorry, too.'

'Well, Penelope came to their assistance and I believe they have since found what they were looking for,' she went on smugly. 'So all has ended well.'

Evie found a smile. 'I am so glad Miss Poindexter was able to succeed where I failed, Mrs Grieves. I'm afraid the spirits are not always as helpful as they could be and Mrs Beatson was particularly difficult.'

'Well, Penelope has so much more experience than you, my dear.'

Honora Stubbs peered around the door in her sensible brown skirt and matching jacket. 'Ah, there you are, dear,' said Leila Grieves. 'Do take Mr Roxburgh and Miss Woodward to their rooms now.'

Honora smiled brightly, her round face fresh and innocent. 'This way, please. Your luggage has been taken up already.' Judging by her eager expression, Evie fully expected Honora to have carried the bags all the way upstairs by herself. Was she really so pleased with her lot in life? Was working for the Grieves family as wonderful as she made it out?

Evie did not think Leila would be an easy employer however elegant and genteel she was. There was something in her eyes, something cold, that made Evie consider turning tail.

As if he sensed her feelings, Daniel took her arm as they followed the housekeeper towards the staircase. He raised his eyebrows at her silently asking what the matter was, but Evie shook her head. Now was not the time to discuss it.

There were three sections to the staircase, set at right angles to each other, and quite steep. A large stained glass window filled the wall on the first landing. It depicted a rustic scene which on closer examination turned out to be of gold miners digging in a bare and mangled landscape.

'Mr Grieves liked to be reminded of the origins of his fortune,' Honora said brightly, noting their interest. 'He strongly believed that money earned was far more valuable than money inherited.'

Daniel's reply was lost in a loud cry echoing from the floor above. A door slammed. Surprised, Evie turned her head as they reached the middle landing, but she could only see the base of the wooden balustrade across the upper floor.

Someone was in a great hurry.

The footsteps were running in their direction, and they would soon head downstairs. A child, perhaps? But as far as she knew there were no children at Blue Waters. Besides, the footsteps did not sound like those of a child.

Honora was still chatting away. 'There are ten guests at Blue Waters for the weekend, excluding the family.'

Ah, perhaps it was an over-exuberant guest. But why were Honora and Daniel ignoring the footsteps? They were getting closer. Why didn't they look up or make some comment. Something cold slid across Evie's warm skin, but she chastised herself. They hadn't even started yet. There was no need to be afraid until the performance began, and even then she was determined to control it.

There would, Daniel assured her, be no repeat of what had happened at the Beatsons'. He would be watching her to make certain of it. And Evie told herself she believed him.

They were almost at the top of the staircase, and the upper landing had begun to come into view through the carved balustrade. It was wide and long and stretched back towards a wall, a *blue wall*.

Evie blinked and her steps faltered. There was an enormous window set into the wall and a vast expanse of blue, blue sky. The colour seemed unvarying, but as she stared she saw the coloured glass birds that appeared to flutter and soar.

The blue.

She heard her own gasp. The blue was real? How could that be? She had never thought, even in her wildest nightmares, that the blue could be *real*.

Her hand found Daniel's and her head was full of noise.

Quiet, you must be very very quiet . . . Not a peep from you, Evangeline . . .

She felt off balance, as if she were falling, even though her feet were perfectly flat on the stairs. Falling down, down into nothingness, into darkness. Into the blue.

'Evie?' Daniel, urgent, his fingers bruising her own. 'Evie, are you all right?'

Her eyes were riveted to the blue window, as she came up the last few steps and stood before it. She felt it tugging at her, trying to swallow her whole, but she held firm.

'I'm perfectly all right, thank you, Daniel.' Her voice was oddly calm and brittle. The voice of the child-Evie who had learned through years of punishment to show nothing. The child had returned and opened the door on the past.

Evie's bedroom wasn't close to the blue window, but in a quiet corridor on the eastern side of the house. She was grateful for that, even though the carved wooden panelling gave the room a sombre feel. A second door led into a bathroom with a sunken marble bath. Luxurious, if you didn't look too closely at the shabby decor.

Her luggage had been placed on the floor by the double bed. A delicate porcelain vase held fresh flowers and a jug offered cool water. Evie filled a glass, her hands still violently shaking. Somehow she had thanked Honora and assured Daniel again that she was fine and closed the door on their curious faces. Now she stood, gulping the water and staring blindly from the open glass doors leading onto the little iron balcony. She wondered if she were losing her mind.

Again.

The blue was real. It existed. The window had been there, almost exactly as she had always visualised it. The wall of sky and the flying glass birds.

She had heard Honora explaining that Sir Henry had commissioned the window in 1900 at great expense. It was meant to represent summer and to remind him of his home in Yorkshire.

The humming inside her head was making her feel nauseous. Confused. The window was real, it existed. It wasn't a lie, as her father had tried to make her believe, or the product of a disturbed childish mind. She did not understand it and right now she didn't have time to try. Daniel needed her to be at her best and she could not perform if she was distracted by this discovery.

Later. I will think about it later. When I am safe at home with Jimmy and Gwen. In Earle Street.

Except that Earle Street was no longer safe. Gunner Connor wanted his money and he could come to get it at any time. And that was Billy's fault.

Slowly the humming stopped and her hands steadied. There were more important things than the blue. She finished drinking, then walked out onto the balcony and focused on the view. She began to list in her mind what she could see to regain her tranquillity. It was an old trick and she hadn't had to use it in many years, but it still worked.

To her right was a large glass and iron conservatory and inside a rose garden encircled a fountain, its bushes covered in voluptuous blooms. A small tan terrier ran yapping along a wide gravel walk and disappeared through an archway laden with honeysuckle. A rough line of mature trees sheltered this part of the garden from the elements and from prying eyes.

Once, she supposed, Sir Henry Grieves had been a king in his castle. He had strutted the halls of Blue Waters, taken its women and done very much as he pleased. Now he was dead and, soon, she had to make him speak again.

The prospect was not one she relished, but she had faced worse and survived.

Much calmer now, she went over again in her mind what Daniel had already told her about the Grieves family. Leila was Henry's second wife and the first had died after giving birth to Raymond in 1874. Leila had one son, Leo, born in 1880, exactly nine months after she married. There was a six-year gap between the two brothers. Raymond had recently married an actress some fifteen years younger than himself, but Leo, now in his late forties, was still a bachelor. Neither of the sons had children and perhaps they never would. Henry Grieves had built an empire fit for a dynasty – but all for nothing.

The terrier was back and still yapping. A woman followed it, a shadowy form in the fading light, her dress brushing her ankles in soft folds and flounces. Her laugh sliced through the quiet and with a start Evie recognised Diana Ashman from Muriel Nelson's cocktail party. Behind her, Leo was leaning against the arch, his hands in his pockets and his ankles crossed. His voice drifted up to Evie's balcony in a low murmur. Diana laughed again and turned to him, pressing her palms against his chest. He put his arms around her and they vanished into the scented shadows. But not before Evie had recognised the intensity of their embrace.

They were lovers.

The only trouble was that Diana was the very actress that Raymond Grieves had so recently married.

A knock on her door startled her. It was Daniel. His confident smile was gone and though he was still his usual charismatic self, there was a restless brooding in his eyes that told her how worried he was. He prowled around her room, peering into the wardrobe and the bathroom, opening drawers, snooping. She watched him irritably, but he didn't seem to notice. Eventually she sat on her bed, crossed her legs and waited for him to tell her whatever it was he had come to say.

'What did Mrs Grieves mean by with that comment about Penelope Poindexter?'

He'd stopped in front of her. Evie looked up into his dark eyes and shrugged. 'Just letting us know she understands about these things.'

'Do you think she's onto us?'

She shook her head. 'If she was, why would she

have asked us for the weekend?'

'To make bloody fools of us.'

'No, I think she's curious. Perhaps Penelope wasn't as forthcoming about Blue Waters as she would have liked. We'll have to outshine her and give a five-star performance.'

Daniel frowned. He looked down at her knee, where the hem of her skirt had ridden up. His expression altered and he quickly looked away. 'You'd better change your clothes. Go over your lines.'

'I know my lines. Relax.'

'You're still angry about Billy, aren't you?'

She shrugged. 'You should have told me.'

'It was between Billy and me. Why should I have told you? So that you could repay his debts for the rest of your life at two shillings a week?'

It sounded ridiculous when he said it like that and Evie knew she was being unreasonable, but she couldn't help it. Daniel's unexpected sacrifice had thrown her off balance. She had thought she knew him and now she was beginning to wonder if she knew him at all. Besides, her anger was fading, shifting, hovering above the person who actually deserved to feel the weight of it. Billy.

She felt uncomfortable about hating Billy, even a little bit. It was as if Daniel and he were no longer the men she had thought them, as if she had caught sight of them through a fairground mirror and their reflections were distorted. They were the same people, but . . . different. And now she was going to have to get to know them all over again.

'What was all that about on the landing?'

She could feel Daniel trying to see beneath her

mask, but she wouldn't look at him. 'I felt a little dizzy. Not enough sleep – and the heat. Who knows?'

'I need to know. I can't cover for you if I don't know what's going on.'

'Nothing's going on.'

'Evie –'

'Daniel, this time if I need your help I'll let you know.'

It wasn't a very nice thing to say, but she couldn't help it.

When the door closed behind him, she lay back on the bed her arms outstretched and body limp. She felt infinitely weary. What was the point in telling Daniel about the blue and the voices? He wouldn't understand what was happening any more than she did. She needed to stay calm, just until this was over. And afterwards - well, there were questions that needed to be answered, questions that should have been answered long ago. And this time she wasn't going to run away from them.

CHAPTER 7

❦

THE DINING ROOM WAS LIT by a magnificent chandelier. The milky light flattered the women in their beaded evening dresses and their glittering jewellery, while the men in their traditional black and white were stark by contrast. Evie felt as if she'd stepped into another world, and one that wasn't quite real to her. But as she took her place and slipped on Evangeline Woodward's enigmatic mask, her confidence began to return.

'Miss Woodward.' Swathed in lavender silk, with diamonds at her throat Leila Grieves was gracious. 'You've met my son, Leo? And this is my step-son, Raymond.'

Raymond was dapper enough, but his smile wasn't as friendly as Leo's, and there was an impatience in his blue eyes, as if this was an occasion he would much rather forego. His hair was iron-grey and he wore it long in a flamboyant manner, rather like a Russian ballet dancer.

Raymond was certainly very different from the fair smiling Leo, and Evie did not think he would be as tolerant of his step-mother's spiritual leanings.

But Leila hadn't finished her introductions. 'And this is Raymond's wife, Diana.'

It was Diana Ashman, pale and sleek in a white dress with very thin straps. Evie remembered the scene she had witnessed earlier on in the garden. Did Raymond know that his wife and brother were having an affair? Did he care? Perhaps their marriage was simply one in name only, to please the fans who wanted to believe Diana was a good little wife to her film-maker husband. It was certainly a match made in publicity heaven.

'We've already met,' Diana announced with her professional smile. 'At Muriel's.'

Muriel and her husband were also there as guests, although Muriel appeared edgy, certainly not the wholehearted enthusiast she had been before her own ghostly experience. Evie couldn't blame her. It was never nice to be abused by a deceased spouse. Kenneth Nelson oozed charm, but again it left her cold. The other guests were strangers and included a couple of Leila Grieves's friends and several film cronies of Raymond's, whose faces she vaguely recognised.

Honora supervised the meal, ordering the servants about as if she were a *maitre d'*. They ate well, although Diana left most of her food on her plate. Perhaps her sleek figure was not natural, but demanded sacrifice, or perhaps she was just too nervous to eat. Evie could not help but notice her anxious glances towards Leo, who was flirting with one of the guests, and her brittle laughter whenever he was near her. You didn't need to be a genius to realise that Diana was desperately in love with Leo and at the same time desperately insecure.

Daniel was involved in a political discussion. Evie half listened as he skated over Prime Minister Bruce's treatment of the unions and his inability to break their grip on the country.

'The ordinary man doesn't respect him,' Leo put in. 'No one can hope to lead a country without the respect of its people. A leader must be strong.'

'Leo should know,' Diana teased. 'Did you know that he was a war hero?'

'Diana, please.' Leo looked genuinely embarrassed. 'That's ancient history.'

'No, no, the story must be told,' she insisted. Centre stage, for Diana, was obviously the natural place to be. 'Leo held off a German patrol. He and his men fought hand-to-hand through some dreary French forest. Luckily for him, he won. But why don't you ever wear your medal, Leo?'

'Yes,' his mother added from her seat at the head of the table. 'Why *don't* you wear it? Your father would have been so proud of you.'

'All of the men that day were heroes,' Leo reminded her.

'But they didn't all get medals,' she countered. 'You were their commanding officer. You told them what to do.'

'Leo's very good at telling people what to do,' Diana said smugly. 'That's because he doesn't actually order them about; he persuades them, gently, into thinking it was what they really wanted to do in the first place!'

Evie could not help but glance at Raymond, to see what he was feeling. But Raymond was leaning across to converse with some of his film friends, either ignoring Diana's behaviour or unaware of it.

'If Raymond had a medal, I'm sure he'd wear it. Wouldn't you, darling?'

Because she was watching him, Evie caught the grimace on Raymond's face, the tightening of his lips. Not quite so unaware after all, it seemed.

'He'd make a moving picture about it.' Leo gave his brother a friendly smile. 'It's all grist to Raymond's mill. Isn't it, brother?'

'Do you mean the way in which Raymond used what happened to you, Leo, in that scene in "Bushland Lady"?' Muriel called out excitedly. 'When the brothers fight and one of them falls and twists his leg, and he's never able to walk properly again, and . . .' She seemed to realise that what she was saying was not being received well and stopped.

Raymond had lowered his lids and was poking at his meal with his fork. Leila looked frozen at the head of the table. Evie heard Muriel murmur an aside to her husband. 'I didn't know it wasn't supposed to be mentioned! How can one possibly remember these things?'

It was Leila Grieves who broke the uncomfortable silence. 'Leo, I want you to tell Mr Roxburgh about your father's life.'

'Oh, but is that wise?' Diana couldn't help herself.

Leila gave her a hard look. 'What do you mean, Diana?'

'Well . . .' Diana took a deep breath, about to give voice to what everyone else was thinking.

But surprisingly it was Raymond who stepped in and defused the situation. 'I think what Diana meant, Leila, was that we would be giving the game away if we told Mr Roxburgh too much about ourselves beforehand. After all, it's his job to find out for himself, isn't it?'

She waved a beringed hand. 'I shall know if they're fakes.'

There was plenty of laughter around the table.

Daniel gave her his most charming smile. 'Mrs Grieves, I assure you that Evie and I are very serious about what we do. Prepare to be amazed.'

She smiled back as if she couldn't help it. 'I am very much looking forward to being amazed, Mr Roxburgh.'

Honora was supervising the serving of the dessert. Just then the girl glanced towards the table and there was something furtive in the movement. Evie, who was practised in uncovering secrets, wondered whether Honora had a lover among the guests. Perhaps someone of whom Leila would not approve of? Not that Honora was a servant, exactly, but Leila had been a servant once herself and she might be more rigid in her observance of class boundaries because of it.

Know your place had been one of her father's favourite sayings. Evie wondered what he would think if he could see her now. Her mother had barely mentioned his name after they escaped, but Evie had known he was often in her mind. He was like a shadow over their lives, and when her mother died, Evie was determined to shake him off. By then she was a grown woman, working and living her own life. She absolutely refused to be afraid of an old man, no matter how savage he had been in his treatment of her when she was child.

But now she found she was thinking of him more than ever. The blue and the Frenchwoman and her father, the voices from her childhood that had haunted her and made her life a misery. They were all coming back and she seemed helpless to stop them.

There was a clatter of running steps and she glanced at the door. It was ajar, ready for the exodus of servants back to wherever they had come from. A woman stood in the shadows. She didn't look as if she had been running. There was a ripple of silver as she moved, turning her face away from Evie, and her hair looked bright and untidy. But there was something in the way she stood, so silent in the gloom, that struck Evie as odd.

Honora fussed about. A large ice sculpture, a replica of Blue Waters, had been carried in on a tray. It was already dripping. The guests applauded politely, but Evie thought the creator had taken some liberties with the architecture – surely the tower wasn't that tall, or the windows that large?

The woman in the silver dress had moved. She was inside the room now and standing slightly apart from a group of uniformed girls who were lined up in a row, listening to Honora explain the finer details of the sculpture. She still had her head turned from Evie, but she wore a silver dress, which was long and old-fashioned in design, with a train. Puzzled, Evie also noticed it was somewhat grubby, as if she had been walking around outside in it. She tried to catch Daniel's eye, wondering if he too had noticed the woman, but he was involved in a conversation with Diana Ashman-Grieves.

'Well, it's so much claptrap!' Diana said in a loud voice. 'I know it was all the rage for the Victorians, but in these modern times who on earth believes in ghosts?'

'Diana!' cried Muriel. 'You were there when Howard came to us. You spoke with him. You distinctly said that he'd never been in better form. How can you doubt it now?'

Diana shrugged one slim shoulder and sipped her drink. She was already inebriated. She had clearly been drinking long before she came down to dinner.

'All done with mirrors, darling,' Diana said now. 'Ask gorgeous Daniel here, except I'm sure he won't be revealing his secrets to us.'

Leila gave Evie a thin smile. 'My daughter-in-law professes to be a skeptic, Miss Woodward. She wasn't brought up on spiritualism as I was. So you must convince her otherwise.'

'Yes, Miss Woodward,' Diana drawled, 'do try. Can we expect another visit from Howard?'

'Diana.' Raymond's voice was restrained but steely. His wife tilted her head towards him and gave him her bright smile.

Honora had finished overseeing the removal of the debris from the earlier courses and the servants hurried out. Again Evie caught sight of the woman in the silver dress over by the sideboard. She had her back to the table and as Evie's gaze slid over her, the streaks of dirt on her silver train were unmistakable. There was even a tear in one corner. It was very odd.

She glanced about, wondering why no one else thought it strange. No one had spoken to the woman, and yet she was clearly not a servant. An eccentric relative perhaps? A mad aunt they kept locked in the tower and tried their best to ignore?

Except that this woman was young. Evie had not seen her face, but she carried herself like a young woman.

Muriel was waffling on about a function she had attended the night before, while Kenneth Nelson smiled his gigolo smile. Evie tried to concentrate, but felt her gaze sliding back once more to the woman in the silver dress. It was as if she was familiar, and yet she was certain she had never seen the woman before.

Who was she?

She appeared to be trying to decide between the champagne and the red wine as her hand hovered first over one and then the other. Loud laughter from those around her momentarily distracted Evie and when she glanced up again it was to see that the woman was now standing by the door. Evie had to crane her neck slightly, to see around Leo Grieves's blonde head. In the doorway, the strange woman half-turned, slowly, consciously, in the manner of one who is fully aware of being observed. She gave a brief, sly glance back into the room.

Fair hair, yellow as butter, hung untidily about her face. Her skin was pale, with hectic circles of red on her cheeks, and there was a thick gold chain about her neck, weighed down by the biggest ruby Evie had ever seen. The setting for the stone looked elaborate and old fashioned, the sort beloved by the Victorians.

The woman's sly glance had passed over the guests seated at the table, until it reached Evie. And there it stopped and fixed. Evie felt it attach itself like a cold breeze to her skin. Pale eyes in a narrow white face. There was no kindness, no shy friendliness, only a sort of furtive watching. She shuddered as the door swung closed and the woman was gone.

'Evie?'

She blinked and Daniel's face came into focus. He nodded in Leo's direction.

'I'm sorry to interrupt your thoughts, Miss Woodward,' Leo said apologetically. 'You were far away.'

'Oh. I was . . . casting a psychic net, Mr Grieves.'

It was one of Daniel's sayings and always sounded impressive.

Leo didn't seem impressed, however. For a moment she thought he was going to laugh in her face, but the impression was gone as quickly, and was replaced by his kindly smile.

Diana smirked. 'A trance, Miss Woodward? Do tell us what you've just seen.'

Evie felt jolted by the compelling look the stranger had given her, but now was not the time to give herself away. 'Nothing specific,' she said frankly. 'Tomorrow I think I will know more.'

Leila began to tell everyone what Penelope Poindexter thought about trances, and Evie pretended to pay attention. Other conversations resumed and the meal ended at last. The women retired in the old manner to a sitting room, while the men remained in the dining room with their drink and tobacco. 'I know it is seldom done these days,' Leila said, when Diana protested, 'but I prefer it. I cannot abide cigar smoke.'

Evie wandered over to an alcove, where the large window had been thrown open to the faint evening breeze. Somewhere a gardenia breathed out its almost sickly sweet scent and crickets called to each other from below the flagged terrace. There was a rustle in the bank of shrubs that jutted out into the lawn and Evie saw a tail waving. A cat was hunting for its supper.

Her head was humming again, as if there was something dangerous close by. But she forced herself to relax, to think about what she was here for and what she had to do. She had learned a lot tonight, much of it useful. But she had to find a chance to share it with Daniel, so that they could plan the detail of their performance tomorrow.

'Miss Woodward!' Leila called her back into the room. The elderly woman was holding court from an ornate chair and the similarity to a throne was not lost on Evie.

'I wanted to show you my husband,' Leila said and gestured to the portrait hanging on the wall behind her. 'There he is, in his prime. Henry wasn't young when I married him, but he was still handsome.'

The man in the painting was striking rather than handsome. He had a fleshy face with overlarge features and a hard, blunt mouth. No one could go from rags to riches as Henry Grieves had done without trampling upon other folk along the way, but Henry did not look as if it had bothered him much.

'I am sure he was a wonderful character,' Evie said politely. 'He looks a little like Leo, doesn't he?'

Leila studied her for a moment with an odd look in her eyes. 'Raymond takes after his mother,' she replied at last. 'And yes, you are right, there is more of Henry in Leo than in his brother.'

'What would Henry think of you selling Blue Waters?' Diana mused. She was still sipping champagne and ignoring the coffee Honora had brought in on the tray.

'He would certainly understand that the day for such extravagances has passed,' Leila replied quietly. 'Henry was a practical man and he always did what had to be done, no matter how difficult it was. He would agree that to sell is the only sensible course of action.'

Evie wondered if Leila was right. Surely Blue Waters had been Henry's crowning glory, the pinnacle of his life's achievements. Far from being sensible, he was probably seething at the prospect of their selling it. Daniel was right. They could make quite a bit of mileage out of Henry's restless spirit.

The men joined them soon after. Daniel gave her a questioning look, but she smiled to reassure him. Raymond cast up his eyes when he saw his wife weaving towards the drinks trolley and came to take her arm. He leaned close, speaking to her in a tense whisper, but she laughed as though he'd made a joke. Raymond wasn't smiling.

She was certainly in a state. Leo, hovering near the coffee tray with Muriel and Honora, judiciously ignored his brother and sister-in-law arguing. If she had not been fairly certain it was so, Evie would never have believed at this moment that they were lovers. As she watched, Leo said something to Honora and gave her a friendly smile. The girl flushed rosily, her dark eyes shining.

'Will you and Miss Woodward walk over the house tomorrow and look for ghosts?' Muriel called to Daniel. 'As you did at my place?'

'Perhaps they can do an exorcism,' Diana mocked, slurring her words. 'Send old Henry to hell.' She laughed loudly and there were some shocked echoes, but most of the people in the room turned to Leila for their cue.

Her face was like stone. 'Your wife is drunk, Raymond. I think you should take her to bed.'

At once Raymond grasped Diana's arm and began to walk her to the door. 'Come on, Diana,' he said sharply. He looked angry and embarrassed. Evie thought that, with a wife like this, embarrassment was probably Raymond's constant companion. Hadn't he realised that before he married her?

Diana gave her husband a mutinous look, but she was too drunk to protest much. Once the door had closed on them, the atmosphere seemed to lighten. Looking about her, Leila seemed to agree. 'I think the sooner we all forget about Diana the better,' she said firmly. 'I hope your newspaper will not print anything about her little problem, Muriel.'

'Oh no, of course not, Leila!' Muriel twittered. 'Wouldn't dream of it.'

'I'm glad to hear it.'

'Little problem,' Daniel murmured, raising his eyebrows, as he followed Evie upstairs to their rooms some time later. 'The woman is a drunk.'

'I was wondering why Raymond married her. Surely he knew? They've worked together.'

'Perhaps it was good publicity.' He shrugged, saying aloud what she had already thought. 'Or maybe Raymond inherits all Henry's worldly goods when Leila dies, and Diana wants the money.'

'I don't think Leila would let that happen.'

'Maybe not. But how have they kept Diana's drinking quiet? I haven't seen a whisper of it any-where.'

'Leila could keep anything quiet,' Evie retorted. 'There's something about her. I wouldn't want to cross her, you know.'

He took her arm in his and she left it there. They were near the upper landing. 'Just be careful what Henry says tomorrow. Fruity but endearing, Evie. Nothing slanderous. Let's not allow it to get out of hand, as you did with Howard. We want to please Leila; not have her sue us.'

The blue window was backed by the dark night sky, turning the colours muted. Evie felt her heart quicken, although this time she didn't feel as if she was going to faint. She was getting used to it. Now, if she could just begin to understand it . . .

'Is there something going on between Diana and Leo?' she made herself say. 'I think they're lovers.'

'If they are, then he's not serious about it. He flirts with everyone.'

'So does she.'

'But *she* does it to make Leo jealous.'

She smiled. 'Yes, you're right.'

'A bit of favouritism there, too. Leo's clearly the golden boy. It must have been hell growing up with Leila for a step-mother and Leo for a brother. I'd feel sorry for Raymond, if he wasn't such an arrogant bastard.'

'Yes, it's difficult to feel sorry for a man who curls his hair.'

Daniel laughed.

They had reached the junction of two corridors:

her room was down one and his down the other.

'What was it that Muriel blurted out – about the two brothers fighting? The scene that Raymond evidently stole for his picture?'

Daniel grimaced. 'When they were boys, Raymond and Leo fought, and Leo fell down the stairs. An accident, naturally.'

'Naturally.'

'But Leo broke his leg pretty badly and it never healed. That's why he limps.'

'I thought it was probably an injury from the war. How did he join the army then? Doesn't a soldier have to be sound in both mind and body?'

'He was an officer and times were desperate. Maybe Leila pulled some strings. Anyway, he justified his place, surely, with the medal. Don't you like Leo?'

She did. How could she not like someone as handsome and friendly as Leo Grieves? He didn't seem to have a nasty bone in his body, unlike his mother. A shame he couldn't leave Diana alone; their affair probably wasn't helping her current state.

'He smiles too much,' she teased.

But he wasn't going to be amused and gave her one of his serious looks.

'Will you be all right alone?'

What did he want to do – sit up with her and play cards? She met his eyes without flinching. 'Of course,' she said brightly, putting on the brave face she had worn most of her life. Somewhere a door slammed, she jumped and the brave face slipped.

'Evie?'

'Good night, Daniel.'

He was watching her, but she didn't turn back. No need to let him know just how she was feeling. No need for him to know she was already falling apart.

❦

A breeze, faint but pleasant, stirred the warm air in Evie's room. She lay in the darkness staring at the open windows and out beyond the dark silhouette of the balcony's iron railing. Voices drifted up from somewhere and just a whisper of music. She allowed her eyes to close and the feeling of peace to steal over her.

A memory of the woman in the silver dress touched her thoughts, and with it a sense of dread, as though once more something from the shadows was creeping up on her.

Quiet, you must be very very quiet . . . Not a peep from you, Evangeline . . .

Again, the words popped into her head. She longed to press her fingers into her ears to stop them, even when she knew the voice came from inside.

The music kept wafting up from below. A piano. It soothed her. With her eyes closed she strained to make out the tune, anything to take her mind off herself. But already it had stopped and now there was only silence. She sighed and her thoughts turned again to the following day and her performance. It would need to be spectacular to satisfy Leila Grieves and outdo the infallible Penelope Poindexter. But not so spectacular that Leila would order them to leave and refuse to pay their fee.

She thought of Jimmy and Gwen at home in Earle Street. She thought of Daniel paying off Billy's debts and never saying a word. Of Daniel meeting her at the tram stop that cold day, buying her hot tea and her favourite sultana cake, and offering her this job. What if she had laughed and said, no, she couldn't possibly. The Frenchwoman would never have found her and she would never have come to Blue Waters and seen that the blue was real. But then what would have happened to Daniel and Billy's debts? At times, so much in life hung on a simple yes or no.

She slept.

The nightmare crept so gently into her dreams that at first she did not realise what it was. There were birds floating in that impossibly blue sky and their songs rose separately and yet together, as if from a choir. She stood on the upper landing and watched the birds fly within their prison of blue glass. As they turned and soared, their feathers glistened.

They were so beautiful.

The blue was a good thing, she told herself. *There was nothing to be afraid of here. It wasn't the blue she should be afraid of . . .*

Someone was watching her. She felt it like a finger brushing against her skin, very softly, over and over, until she could no longer ignore it. Slowly her attention was diverted from the birds. Someone was behind her.

She turned around.

The woman in the silver dress stood there. She was even dirtier and more unkempt than she had been in the dining room. Her hair hung down, curling against those hectic cheeks, while streaks of soil ran in the creases on her skirts, and her hands were scratched and bleeding. The big ruby gleamed balefully between her breasts.

'Who are you?' Evie knew she had spoken the words, but could not hear them. 'What do you want?'

That sly glance again, face half-turned away, eyes veiled beneath gold lashes. A shiver overtook Evie, and in that moment she became aware of the stillness about her, the emptiness of the house. She and the woman in the silver dress were alone.

'You're hurt,' Evie offered, gesturing to the torn hands.

The woman muttered something, a few words under her breath and her voice seemed deep, almost rough.

'What is it? What did you say?'

'*Au secours.* Help me, Evangeline.'

The voice, the French, suddenly everything fell together and made sense.

This woman in her grubby silver finery was the nightmare of her childhood made flesh. The Frenchwoman, who had followed her and lost her and now had found her again.

The fear was overpowering.

The Frenchwoman came forward, her silver dress rustling like the birds in the blue glass sky. She reached out her bleeding hands and said, 'Hide, hide,' in her roughened voice.

Evie screamed.

In her dream she turned and ran.

Down the stairs, stumbling, hands clutching the

balustrade. The entrance hall was empty but she paused on the last step her head turning from side to side as she looked for Daniel. Panting, letting her heart slow and her breathing regain some normality. The Frenchwoman was here and she had a face. And that was very bad.

But she could bear it. She could, she could, just as she had always been able to when she was a child.

Above her she heard footsteps and shivered violently. The grate of a shoe on wood fell like a shadow across her mind. At the same moment someone came down the first step. Someone with a man's shape. The hunter was coming and this time it was *Evie* who was the prey.

The scream ripped out of her throat. She couldn't prevent it. She fell out of her bed and began to scramble to the door, still screaming.

The door banged open and she screamed again.

'Evie! Evie, for Christ's sake, Evie!' It was Daniel, shaking her awake, his arms warm and solid and real.

She clung to him. She heard Raymond's voice and then Honora's asking questions and expressing concerned. But Daniel was reassuring them and, eventually, they were alone.

'She was here. She lives here,' Evie whispered, as if the Frenchwoman would hear her if she spoke too loudly.

'There's no one here,' Daniel insisted. He lifted her head and forced her to look at him. He was pale and haggard, his beard a dark shadow on his jaw but his paisley dressing gown was soft against her bare arms. 'See? Evie, there's no one there.'

The ceiling light was on. The room was definitely empty, and her eyes filled with tears as they scanned the tumbled bed and the deserted balcony.

'Come on, look around for yourself. There's no one here.'

Tentatively she left the shelter of his arm and crept about the room. But he was right. Everything was as she had left it. The Frenchwoman had gone again, but she knew that this time she hadn't gone very far.

Daniel sat on the edge of the bed, watching her.

'Well?' he demanded.

She sighed. 'I'm sorry. I had a nightmare. Did everyone hear me?'

'They could have heard you out on the bay.'

She wanted to laugh, to please him, but it was beyond her. She wrapped her arms about herself and shuddered.

'Evie . . . Come on. We'll go home.'

'Daniel –'

'I was wrong to persuade you to come. You didn't want to. So we'll make our excuses and leave.'

She wanted to do that more than anything, to climb into Daniel's car and drive far away. To leave behind Blue Waters with its odd feelings and memories and the Frenchwoman in her silver shroud and the faceless man who was following her.

But how could she leave when their whole future depended on staying? Leila's money would buy them both their freedom. She *had* to see it through and play her part.

She shuddered again. 'No,' she managed. It was loud, strong. 'No,' she said again and felt better for it. These were childhood fears, weren't they? Tricks of the mind. And yet the blue was no trick; it was real. Could the Frenchwoman be real, too? It was better not to think about that, not now. Think of Jimmy, she told herself sternly. Think of Jimmy leaving Earle Street and living somewhere pleasant. Think of a garden and perhaps a puppy and Gwen's smile.

'I have to finish this,' she said quietly. She came and sat down beside him and the mattress gave way so that their bodies pressed together. It was comforting to feel him there, and for once she did not try and move away. 'I can do it, Daniel. One last time.'

He glanced at her sideways, his dark eyes sliding over her cheek, as if trying to gauge just how crazy she was. She even managed a smile at the thought.

'Was it this Frenchwoman you've been on about?' he asked her. 'Is that what frightened you?'

Evie shook her head, and then again for good measure. 'I'll be all right.'

'Evie . . .'

'I was thinking,' she hurried on, so that he couldn't ask more questions. 'I can use this dream. If I was really a spirit hunter I would see things like that. People who weren't really there. I'll play it up tomorrow. A woman in a silver dress who has something to tell me.'

She stared into his eyes, thinking that he had to know how frightened she was. He had to.

'All right,' he said slowly. 'We can do that.' He seemed to be choosing his words carefully. 'Why don't you tell me about her now, this woman in the silver dress? Just so I'm ready.'

Tell him? Speak of it aloud? Fear froze her. But then she thought, Why not? Telling Daniel would be liberating, when all the time she would be sharing one of her darkest secrets with him. That was to say, if her tongue would obey her.

'She's w-wearing a s-silver dress,' she stammered. 'It's torn and dirty. She has blonde hair. She's pretty – sort of – though her face is too thin and too long for real beauty. And she has a ruby necklace around her neck, set in pearls, on a gold chain. It looks valuable, old. Maybe she stole it – I don't think it's hers, Daniel.'

He was still watching her and searching her face for clues. Evie wished she could read his mind, or maybe it was better that she couldn't.

'We can work on it,' he said at last. 'If you're sure you want to go ahead with this.'

She nodded. Her body felt so weary and ached as if she'd been hurt. Despite the warm night, she was cold. Her hair hung loose down her back, tangled and darkened with perspiration. Her nightgown didn't hide much. All this time his gaze had stayed on her face and he hadn't tried a thing. He'd been a gentleman.

Honourable.

There was that word again. It no longer seemed incongruous. Daniel was an honourable man. He mightn't be safe, like Billy – like she'd *thought* Billy was – but if there was one person in the world she could rely on in this situation it was Daniel Roxburgh.

He stood up now. 'Get some sleep,' he said gruffly.

She might have laughed at the part he was playing, Daniel as the gentleman, except that she knew now that it wasn't acting. She thought about reaching out and taking his fingers in her own, and wondered what would happen if she did. And then she wondered what would happen if she didn't, and Daniel left her here alone.

It seemed suddenly silly to deny herself the solace – besides it was what they both wanted, wasn't it?

'Daniel,' she murmured softly. 'Daniel, I can't be left. Not tonight.'

He half-smiled. 'I thought you hated me.'

'Oh, no. I don't hate you. I've never hated you. Are you going to say no?'

He looked away briefly. 'I'm not going to say no. Tell me, Evie, why here, why now?'

'Because I need you,' she said simply. 'Maybe I'm being selfish, but that's what I want to be. I can't promise you anything other than here and now. Do you understand that?'

She was being frank with him. How could she look to tomorrow when she didn't know what it would bring? He deserved better than a lie.

He met her searching gaze and smiled. He thought he could change her mind, she realised and she knew she should send him back to his room, now, before it was too late. But she didn't want to and for once she was going to ignore her head and do exactly what her heart told her.

His mouth tasted of whisky and cigarettes and the Grande Ballroom. She felt his beard rasp on her skin, and her fingers slid over the scar on his shoulder where Squizzy Taylor had tried to kill him.

'Please stay with me,' she said against his lips. 'Let's just be Daniel and Evie – nothing more.'

Not Billy's best friend and not Billy's widow.

He laughed with soft self-mockery, as if he knew he was going to stay whatever his own doubts might be.

'Evie,' he whispered, and drew her down onto the bed. 'My Evie.'

And for tonight she was.

CHAPTER 8

𝒞

THE NEXT DAY WAS OVERCAST, the sky heavy steel. The garden beneath Evie's window looked sullen, despite the cream splash of honeysuckle across the arch. She could smell the salt of the bay more strongly now and hear the screech of gulls.

She was up and had dressed early, hiding the dark circles under her eyes with a light dusting of powder, drawing her mouth on with particular care. Her dress was faded rose with a collar of fur and she knew she appeared fashionable and elegant. But inside she felt fragile. As if, like a champagne glass, she might shatter at the slightest bump.

Daniel had stayed with her until dawn. Whether the Frenchwoman had been a dream or a ghost, his presence had been enough to keep her at bay. Evie had felt safe and had managed to sleep. When he left her, she had lain looking out at the sky as it lightened, her mind and body tired, but calm. The terror had gone and only a faint echo of it rang deep in her mind.

She wondered what Jimmy was doing. Was he

holding out his arms to Gwen, demanding to be picked up? Did she smile and hug him and see Billy in his plump sweet face? The dark thought stole into Evie's mind and she was tired and not quick enough to stop it. *Would Gwen see last night as a betrayal of Billy's memory?'*

Last night in Daniel's arms. It had been a revelation, real and intense and immediate. The slight distance she had felt between herself and the world was shattered for once and all, and if things had been different she would want to share the next night with Daniel and the one after that.

But could she really inflict that burden on Billy's mother?

'You're a bad girl, Evie,' her father said, the night she had woken to find him staring down at her. 'A wicked, lying girl.' And later, the last time she had ever seen him, as he stood on the doorstep looking back, 'You deserve everything you get.'

She did not think she had done so badly. The years after she and her mother had run away had been grim, that was true, but they had made a life for themselves. Then she had met Billy and been blessed with Jimmy.

And yet, always, there was that sense of something waiting in the shadows. Of an ominous truth waiting to overwhelm her. She couldn't run away again, but equally she didn't know whether she could stay and fight whatever it was that was coming for her. Could she rely upon Daniel to be by her side, and did she want him there anyway.

The tan terrier was yapping again. Evie went to the balcony and peered down. Leo was standing in the rose garden with Diana Ashman. He bent to scratch the dog's head, retrieved the ball from its jaws and threw it again.

It was a peaceful scene.

So why was Diana crying?

Perhaps Evie made a sound, or perhaps he just sensed her watching him, because Leo glanced up. He looked surprised to see her, but then he lifted a hand in awkward acknowledgement, at the same time stepping in front of Diana to try and hide her from view.

'Miss Woodward, I do hope you're feeling better this morning. No more bad dreams?'

'No, thank you. I am much better. And call me Evie – please.'

Diana had turned away, pretending to unhook her dress from a thorn. Something about her hunched shoulders made Evie's heart ache. Diana was difficult and irritating and she had serious problems, but she was a woman in need of good advice. Evie doubted she would get it from either Leila or Leo. Raymond had come to her rescue at dinner, but even if he did love her, he could only endure so much. Having his nose rubbed in an affair between his wife and his brother had to be the last thing he needed.

Leo was smiling as if nothing was wrong. 'Evie?'

'I prefer it to Evangeline.'

'Ah. But Evangeline Woodward has such a ring to it. Your father named you well.'

If he had named her at all.

It was difficult to hold a conversation with someone on a balcony, and Leo had no intention of trying. With a clap of his hand to his thigh, he limped off down the gravel path, the dog in pursuit. Glancing briefly over her shoulder, Diana followed.

Evie stood and watched them vanish around the corner.

Breakfast was offered in an array of silver plated and covered dishes on the sideboard. Evie chose toast and eggs and tea and saw Daniel was there with Raymond. They were discussing the current state of the moving picture industry and apart from a brief 'Good morning' in her direction, neither man broke off the conversation.

She sat down and gave them a surreptitious glance. Daniel was the same, she thought, and yet different. When he smiled, she found herself thinking: Last night he had kissed her with that mouth. When he drummed his fingers on the table: He had touched her with that hand.

And she had touched him.

There was a dark pleasure in sitting there and remembering, especially since no one else was aware.

Perhaps that was how Diana felt, when she looked at Leo.

'Nothing will ever be the same again,' Raymond was saying. 'When audiences hear the talking pictures from America they won't want to see the old silent ones – no matter how good they are.'

'My husband is all for moving with the times.' Diana's voice startled Evie and she turned and saw the other woman sitting in the window seat, half-hidden by some draperies.

'We already import most of our pictures from America,' Raymond went on passionately. 'We've all but killed off our own industry so that no one

wants to go and see an Australian picture anymore – and even if they want to they don't get
the chance. '"Bushland Lady"' was an exception –
it was made with American money. I have friends
who are brilliant film-makers and can't get work.'

'You can't blame the audience.' Diana yawned.
'Who wants to see kookaburras when they can
watch a gunfight between goodies and baddies in
the old West?'

Raymond made a sound of disgust. 'You can
joke, Diana, but it's your career as well as mine.'

But she didn't seem to be in the mood for seriousness this morning. Her gaze slid to Evie. 'Miss
Woodward looks rather done-in,' she said. 'I would
have come to your aid last night, Evie,' she drawled,
'but I believe Daniel was adamant that he could
comfort you. I imagine he would be very good at
comforting women.'

Daniel looked down at his plate and smiled.

'Perhaps he could give my husband some lessons.'

'Diana, for God's sake,' Raymond burst out. 'Do
you have to be such a bitch?'

'Well, you told me not to drink, darling. You
know what that does to me.'

Raymond rose noisily to his feet, his face twisted
with anger and disgust. 'Do what you like! I've had
enough.'

When he had gone, Diana wandered over to the
sideboard as if nothing had happened and removed
a cigarette from a large silver box. She lit it and
exhaled the smoke thoughtfully into the air. Evie
glanced sideways at Daniel and he raised his eyebrows. His gaze slid down, to her fur collar and
the white skin beneath. He was thinking about last

night, and the intimacy of the moment struck her anew.

'I'm looking forward to your little show today,' Diana said, still in that dull drawling voice, as if all the life had been sucked out of her. 'When does it start? You'll have to wait until Leila's ready, of course, but she isn't a late riser. I'll enjoy seeing you put Penelope Pointdexter's nose out of joint.'

Daniel's voice was polite in reply. 'I believe Miss Poindexter is a respected member of the Spiritualist Movement. There's room enough for us all, you know.'

'She thinks she *is* the Spiritualist Movement. Leila calls herself Penelope's patron.' She paused, stared into space. 'My husband hates her, you know. Leila, I mean. She made his life a misery when he was growing up.'

'He doesn't seem to have done too badly for a deprived child,' Daniel said dryly.

Diana blew smoke at the ceiling and watched it rise. 'Leila always says that Raymond threw Leo down the stairs because he was jealous of him. Raymond says it was an accident. I think there's more to it, but Raymond won't discuss it and Leo just shrugs and says it's in the past and has been forgotten. But he plays on it, you know. He's good at manipulating people like that.'

Voices outside, Muriel's laughter.

'Still,' Diana went on, 'I can feel a certain degree of sympathy for Leila. Can you imagine how it must have been, with a husband like Henry having his hand up every woman's skirt? I believe, as he got older, he used to give her jewellery away to the favourites, in return for –'

'Jewellery?' Evie repeated sharply.

The ruby, in its old fashioned setting, resting around the Frenchwoman's neck. Evie had sensed it didn't belong to her. Had it been a gift from Sir Henry Grieves for favours given? Had the French-woman been one of his women?

'Yes. Money, too, sometimes. Leila was livid, of course. It must have been a relief to her when he died, although she'd never admit it. She's always kept a close eye on Leo − frightened he'll end up like his father, I suppose. Anyway, it was Leo who persuaded Leila to have you both stay for the weekend. He could always persuade her to do any-thing. I think she's secretly hoping you'll make a mess of things.'

'No fear of that, Miss Ashman. Evie and I are good at what we do.' Daniel gave her one of his best smiles.

Diana smiled back at him and blew more smoke into the air. 'I'll just bet you are,' she murmured. 'And do call me Diana, please. We're old friends now, aren't we? I mean to say, you've seen me drunk and I have a fair idea what you were both up to last night, so we have no secrets from one another.'

Muriel had come in, followed by a group of chattering guests.

'Secrets?' she asked, bright eyed. 'Whatever do you mean, Diana? What secrets?'

But Diana only smiled.

❡

Evie did not have to begin her performance that morning after all. The other guests were keen for a stroll along the beach before the rain set in, and after that there was lunch. Leila had instructed Honora to serve the meal in the glass and iron conservatory that Evie could see under her balcony window.

The conservatory was warm and leafy, and the grey sky high above looked far more inviting than it actually was. But there was an earthy smell in here, close and throat-catching, that made Evie hesitate on the doorstep.

Diana tugged at her arm. Her eyes were glittering and it was clear that she had taken a few shots of something since breakfast. Evie wondered if it was just alcohol, or whether Diana had taken to indulging in other drugs. Gunner Connor, she knew, had begun supplying some of the more fashionable Melbourne parties. They thought it was quaint to have a famous underworld figure arrive at their door, but such naivety did not impress Evie. She knew what Connor was really like.

'Now, now, Miss Woodward, come along,' Diana was saying in a sing-song voice. 'Don't refuse at the first jump.'

The long table was spread with china and silverware, flowers and bottles of champagne, and enough food to feed Leila's guests twice over. Honora was in charge, her cheeks a little flushed as she directed the occasion. As she moved past Muriel's husband he brushed her thigh with a languid hand and made her jump. But she simply smiled politely and moved on, when Evie would have been tempted to slap his face.

Diana was still at Evie's side, whispering in her ear. 'God knows how Leila gets Honora to arrange all this for her. That girl is a marvel. And Leila treats her like dirt, too. Jealous, I expect, of her youth. Leila is terrified of old age.'

'Diana, what are you saying?' Leila's eyes narrowed suspiciously at her step-son's wife. There was clearly little love lost between them, and it was Diana who backed down now, meekly taking her seat beside Raymond. He shot her a glance and Evie could see in his face that he knew his wife was drunk again. A bleak despair filled his eyes and then he turned his head away.

Evie could sympathise with Raymond. Clearly he had had the worst of it as a boy. Had he really thrown Leo down the stairs? If it had been Billy and Daniel, then Gwen would have believed Billy whatever the truth. Evie did not put much faith in Leila's assertions that Raymond had been in the wrong.

Something brushed her arm and made her start. She glanced around, but there was no one close by. Leo was smiling at her, his face as warm and welcoming as ever, and she smiled back.

'This was my father's favourite place, Evie,' he said to her above the noise of the guests and the servants moving around, offering food and pouring drinks.

'Perhaps Miss Woodward can feel him among us.' Leila was sitting at the head of the table, her pale eyes darting about, making sure that all was done properly. She came from another age, when people had set aside their very best rooms for guests only, and spent their lives making do in the shabbier back quarters. An age when people believed that the more ostentatious they were, the more important they became to the rest of the world. After all, Sir Henry Grieves had built Blue Waters on those very principles.

There was the public life and the private life and the Grieves family appeared to have been very adept at keeping their private lives hidden.

'I think I can feel Sir Henry here,' Evie said, lifting her own voice above the din.

There was an immediate hush and she hid her smile as so many interested eyes turned towards her. Some were more interested than others, certainly, and some were more cynical, but it didn't matter. As with Raymond and his moving pictures, this was all about entertainment.

'He's wearing a waistcoat with a watch chain. A silver watch chain.' She smiled in the direction of a bank of palms and imagined Henry lurking among the fronds. He would be smirking, observing Honora probably and savouring lecherous thoughts. 'His shoes pinch,' she said suddenly. 'He's too vain to buy a larger size.'

Leila pressed a hand to her heart. 'You are very clever, Miss Woodward,' she said a little breathlessly. 'Not many people knew that about Henry.'

'He doesn't want you to sell the house,' Evie added, and felt Daniel's tension from further down the table. 'He's sad, but he understands the necessity. Times change. He's shaking his head at that, but he knows it's the truth.'

'So glad he's being reasonable,' Diana murmured.

'He's asking . . .' Evie turned her eyes on Raymond and saw him flinch. 'Have you still got the sixpence he gave you?'

Raymond looked startled. 'No,' he said. 'I spent it.'

Evie sighed deeply, her voice growing a little hoarse as it became Henry's. 'My father gave me sixpence when I was a boy. It was the start of my fortune. Where's your fortune, Raymond? You've squandered it, just as you'll squander mine.'

'I have no desire to be like you,' Raymond replied shakily.

'Miss Woodward –' Leila was growing agitated.

'Evie –' So was Daniel.

'Leo still has *his* sixpence, though,' Evie said. 'He likes to save things, don't you, boy? Saves them up. Leo is the keeper of memories.'

Leo laughed. 'You are very good, Evie. Yes, I do still have my sixpence. I keep it for good luck.'

She blinked and put a trembling hand to her eyes. Henry had been strong, a powerful figure in her mind. How had she known about the sixpence? Had Daniel told her? Or had she heard it somewhere else, a long time ago? As usual at such times she could not remember. But it had worked, the family and their friends were impressed – even Leila, who was doing her best to hide it.

Just for a moment Evie had that feeling again, the sensation that she was on the verge of some momentous discovery. But it was gone as swiftly. After she and her mother ran away, she had tried to forget the past. It was better that way, her mother said. So they had pretended that none of it ever happened, that Frederick Woodward had never existed.

Then, after Jimmy was born, Evie had gone back

to the house where she had once lived. It was one of the bravest things she had ever done. She still wasn't sure exactly why she had done it – perhaps to show herself how far she had come, but more likely to show her father that she had survived.

But the house was gone. The entire street had been demolished and left as a jumbled pile of bricks and wood that the horses and carts were already hauling away. A notice board nearby declared that there would be enough new houses built here for a dozen happy families.

Evie had stood, staring at the spot where her home had been and feeling just as flattened. But it made her realise that nothing stayed the same. Life moved on. And so should she.

CHAPTER 9

'ARE YOU READY?' DANIEL WAS watching her. They were together in the music room – taking a moment apart while the family gathered in the hall. It was late afternoon and the time for their real performance had arrived at last.

Muriel and her friends had gone off, preferring to take a drive along the coast – or strongly encouraged by Leila to do so, according to Diana. After lunch, she had suddenly decided that she did not want a gaggle of witnesses and only the family was now to be present for Evie's disclosures.

'Of course I'm ready,' Evie smiled, but suspected she looked pale. She felt even more like that champagne glass, close to breaking. And yet she was determined not to lose her control, not now when so much depended on her.

He touched her arm possessively and she pulled back.

'Daniel, I warned you. You shouldn't think because of last night that anything between us has changed.' His dark eyes narrowed, but she was the one who looked away. 'I needed you and I was grateful. But things are so complicated at the moment. I don't think it would be good for either of us to believe that we could have a happy ending. Not together.'

'Look,' he said quietly, 'I know the way you think. You want to make everything right for Gwen and Jimmy and after that's done you'll think of yourself. You can't live like that, Evie. Sometimes life is a mess, but that doesn't mean you can't be happy in it. I can make you happy.'

'You don't know just how much of a mess my life is,' she sighed. 'I *have* to put Jimmy and Gwen first. I owe that to Billy. They're my family now and I must look after them. You're so self-sufficient, you don't need me. You'll survive long after we're gone.'

'You're wrong,' he retorted. 'I do need you and not just for this.' He swept his arm around at Blue Waters. 'I've wanted you for as long as I can remember, but there was Billy. Billy always came first. Well, Billy's gone, Evie, and I'm still here.'

Should she be afraid? His dark eyes wouldn't leave hers, his expression was focused and determined. The thought of him in her bed every night was good but the days . . . Gwen's anger and Jimmy being pushed and pulled between them, and then the growing burden of her past returning.

'Mr Roxburgh!' Leila's imperious voice broke the spell.

Daniel's fingers gripped her arm a little tightly. 'Come on,' he said. 'Our audience awaits.'

He had sketched the layout of the house, and he spent a moment checking it. Evie waited, a little to the side, quietening her nerves, while Leila stood back observing them with a half-smile, as if she wasn't expecting much. Diana was fidgeting about nervously, while Leo and Raymond stood together, clearly uncomfortable and more like strangers than brothers.

'We'll start here in the entrance hall,' Daniel announced. He had already taken the air temperature and noted it in his book. He was enjoying himself, but Leila was clearly unimpressed. 'Penelope doesn't actually need to take the temperature. She can tell if there is a presence just by reaching out with her mind.'

'Can we get on with it?' Raymond asked. 'Some of us have work to do.'

'Now, now, Raymond – don't you want to speak to your father again?' Diana gave him a bland smile.

'Henry rarely speaks,' Leila said smugly. 'You were exceptionally lucky at lunch. He's only spoken through Penelope twice.'

'That's because she has the face of a horse,' Diana replied. 'Evie is much prettier, more Henry's style. In fact,' and she cast a look at Leila, 'you must have looked very like Evie when you were young, Leila.'

Leila was frozen with fury. It was Leo who made the peace, as usual. He cast Diana a warning glance but tempered it with a smile and slid his arm around his mother's shoulders. 'I'm sure my father will keep his distance from now on. He much prefers Penelope.'

'Oh, Leo,' Diana said, 'you are such a liar.'

This time there was no smile. The look he gave her was as cold as the rain that had begun to fall outside. Maybe there was more to Leo after all than the genial gentleman of the manor.

Raymond took a step closer to his wife. 'Get

on with it,' he said shortly. 'Diana has to be on set tomorrow. I need to sober her up.'

'That's right – "Bushland Hut", isn't it? The sequel to "Bushland Lady". I can just see Diana in an apron, wielding a broom.' Leo laughed good-naturedly, but Raymond ignored him.

In a disorderly group they meandered through the downstairs rooms, pausing occasionally while Leila reminisced. Several times Daniel glanced at Evie, expecting her to begin, but she was finding it difficult. What was once a game had become something far more frightening. When previously she had willingly opened herself to the shadows around her, using Daniel's meticulous research and her own ideas and imagination to create the illusion, now she was afraid.

The Frenchwoman was waiting, and whether she was fantasy or ghost, it was only a matter of time before she found Evie once more.

They had reached the stairs. This was the place, she knew, that she had to fear above all others. On the upper landing, there was a soft cry and a thump. She froze.

'I'm sorry, Mrs Grieves!' Honora's cheerful voice floated down the stairwell. 'I'll get out of your way.'

She flitted past them clutching a variety of dusters and reeking of furniture polish. Evie tried not to laugh with relief and encountered a *what-are-you-doing?* look from Daniel.

'Bear with us,' he said. 'This is a large house.'

'Indeed?' Leila smirked. Penelope was still queen of the spooks as far as she was concerned.

'Evie?' Daniel led her a little away from the others, his hand on the small of her back. 'What's wrong?' he whispered. 'You should have found two spirits by now. Have you forgotten the plan?'

'I'm sorry. I can't seem to concentrate.'

'Do you need a moment to rest?'

She shook her head and her hair slipped free. Before he could stop himself, he reached out and tucked the strands behind her ear. The intimacy of the gesture wasn't lost on the others who couldn't hear them but could certainly see what they were doing.

Leila cleared her throat theatrically. 'If you're quite ready, Miss Woodward?'

Those pale eyes. There was something. Something . . . Evie drew herself up, ignoring her impending sense of dread and pushing aside the little voice that was telling her to run while she still could.

'Quite ready,' she said.

They climbed the stairs and reached the upper landing. There, directly before them, was the great blue window that dominated the corridor. As Evie stepped towards it, her legs a little wobbly, a small bird darted, chirping, above her head. She cried out, covering her hair with her hands, but the bird had already flown, wings beating, into another corridor.

'A sparrow,' Leo said calmly. 'They will get in, no matter how hard we try to prevent them. Are you all right, Evie? It didn't hurt you?'

His eyes, so similar in colour to his mother's, were kind. So unlike Leila's, so unlike the way she imagined Henry's to be. Then why was she so frightened?

'No, I'm all right. Thank you.' But she felt shaken,

off-balance. The humming in her head had come back and with it the voices, so many of them, clamouring to be heard. It was all she could do not to put her fingers in her ears.

There was a sound coming towards them, faint, but growing louder. She turned and stared behind her, but the landing was empty. The sound came again and now it was like harsh breathing. Panting. As if someone was running hard. Evie grasped Daniel's hand. 'Do you hear that?' she whispered. But he didn't. He shook his head, he looked startled – this wasn't in the script. The breathing grew closer, more laboured.

'What is it?' he shot back at her eagerly. 'Describe it. Evie?'

He thought she'd changed the performance. She wanted to tell him that this was no game, but she couldn't. The family was watching her, their faces frozen, waiting.

'Someone's coming,' she managed, her voice edgy. 'Running. Closer now. I-I can't see them.'

'Who are you?' Daniel called, picking up on her urgency and using it to increase the tension. 'Answer me!'

A cold breath puffed in Evie's ear. She flinched suddenly. Her vocal cords, gripped by an iron fist, were no longer her own.

'I see you there,' the voice whispered. 'I see you. Murderer.'

Leila cried out softly, pressing her hand to her lips, but no one else moved.

The locked door in her mind opened and the shadows drew her in. She was back in the past and she was small. Suddenly so small. The space she was in was hardly much bigger. Dark and quiet. Safe. But she knew she must not make any sound or it would be safe no longer.

Not a peep from you, Evangeline . . .

'Please don't hurt me,' she whispered. 'Where are you? Where have you gone?'

'Evie?' Daniel's voice was too far away to be any help. She was alone – or almost – for the French-woman was here, too. The Frenchwoman had come back for her, just as she'd promised all those years ago . . .

Another cold breath in her ear. The French-woman was standing behind her, so close that her skin prickled. Something soft and damp fell onto her shoulder, slipping down to rest against the fur collar of her dress.

Evie's eyes flickered open.

It was a worm, lying on her skin, soft and pink and wriggling.

Before she could scream her disgust, the shadows snatched her again, taking her back. She was being pulled down the stairs, down into the entrance hall. Her feet stumbled, as if she were sleepwalking.

The hall looked different and smelled different. Blue Waters seemed to have come alive around her. It looked as it must have done earlier in the century, when Henry and the family were still in permanent residence. Not the empty shell it was now, but a house full of whispers and secrets.

'When is this?' Evie gasped. Her legs seemed smaller and shorter, a child's legs. She was running to keep up.

1908, the Frenchwoman replied. *It is Sunday, and everyone is gone. We are all alone,* ma petite. *Now come*

. . . quickly.

Cold impatient fingers clasped hers, tugging her brutally onward.

Through the ground floor rooms, each one a blur. Quicker now, running, her heart so loud she could hardly hear the voices humming in her head. The sense that she was being followed was intense, overwhelming.

Hurry, hurry, Evangeline . . .

'Where are you going?' Daniel beside her, his voice low and urgent. 'Evie?'

'To the kitchen stairs,' she said, annoyed that she should have to use her breath to tell him. 'There is a door down there that leads out into the garden.'

Murmurs, a loud complaint, but she did not hear them. The cold fingers were drawing her on, down the narrow stairs. Honora looked up from the old stove, startled, but she did not see her. The door was there, as she had known it would be, but it was closed. She turned around and saw the other door. The door to the tunnel.

It was open and through it came the smell of the sea, so strong, beckoning her.

Gratefully, she went towards it.

Hands came around her, and held her. No, no, this wasn't supposed to happen! She was meant to run down the tunnel, run towards the sea. He wasn't supposed to catch her yet.

She screamed and immediately her throat closed up. Fingers, pressing into her flesh, choking her, throttling her. She fell to her knees on the wooden floor, voices, growing dimmer, darkness closing in. Only the Frenchwoman's voice remained and it too was fading.

Au secours, Evangeline . . .

Evie swallowed and the tightness in her throat loosened slightly. She was lying on a sofa and someone was leaning over her, pressing a glass to her lips. Daniel, she thought, but when she opened her eyes she saw that it was Leo.

He was calm, his gaze remarkably steady, as he helped her to sip. Brandy. She coughed. Her eyes watered.

'Are you all right, Evie?' he said. Then, his voice dropping, 'That was absolutely brilliant . . . However did you manage it?'

She blinked. She was in one of the sitting rooms and there were the others, gathered by the fireplace. The alcohol was warming her, but still she felt dizzy, as if she had woken from a dream too quickly, and her throat ached. There was something niggling at her and she needed to remember. A name, was it? A woman's name?

'You were speaking French,' Leila said accusingly. 'I don't know of anyone French who lived in Blue Waters.'

There was something defiant in her face, but something frightened, too – and suddenly Evie knew.

You're a proper little lady, aren't you?

'It was you,' Evie whispered, amazed and mortified.

'What are you talking about?' Leila said angrily. 'It was me *what?* I don't think I like the way you conduct your business, Miss Woodward. This is not professional.'

'Evie is very sensitive,' Daniel stepped in with a calming smile. 'Sometimes she cannot put a proper distance between herself and the spiritual vibrations she is receiving. I think this Frenchwoman is a very disturbed entity. Evie spoke to me about her last night.'

'Did she indeed?' Leila wasn't to be pacified.

'A silver dress and fair hair, a pale face that is too narrow and too long for real beauty. A ruby around her neck. Does that mean anything to any of you?'

'Christ . . .' Raymond stepped away from the rest of them, shaking his head, as if he wanted to distance himself.

'I don't think I want to hear any more,' Leila went on, reaching out towards Leo. 'This is all too . . . too dramatic. Penelope is never like this.'

Daniel met Evie's eyes. There was something wrong and he knew it. Not just with Evie, but with Leila, too.

'Mother —' Leo took his mother's arm, but she wouldn't be silenced.

'What is it you really want, Miss Woodward?' Leila said, her voice trembling. 'What are you doing here at Blue Waters?'

'Want? I'm sorry.' Evie's voice was hardly above a whisper, and even that made her throat hurt. 'I don't understand.'

'We are here at your invitation,' Daniel cut in smoothly.

'I am no fool,' Leila went on, talking to Evie and ignoring him completely. 'I have dealt with charlatans before.'

Evie looked confused. 'Charlatans? You saw just now what happened. Someone was murdered in your house! Pursued into the tunnel and strangled! I felt it; for a moment I became that person. How can you believe it wasn't true?'

'Easily. You have come to my house, abused my hospitality, lied to me–'

'Leila,' Diana tried, but might just as well not have bothered.

'They're not lies,' Evie said starkly.

She'd been here before. The blue window was real. And she was beginning to remember other things. Her dreams were not dreams at all. They were memories of places and people she once knew.

The realisation was stunning.

'My son has made enquiries about you, Miss Woodward,' Leila went on, her mouth pinched at the edges. Leo shifted from foot to foot, looking absurdly guilty and apologetic, as though he were four rather than forty-eight. 'You are not gifted,' Leila went on. 'You worked in a place called, I believe, the Peking Tea Rooms? And before that you ran away from home because your father was concerned about your state of mind. Your mother was afraid he was going to put you into a hospital for the mentally unsound, so she kidnapped you. You are a charlatan, Miss Woodward. Or, more likely, one of those persons to be pitied, who cannot tell fantasy from fact.'

Evie felt dizzy; she felt as if she could not breathe. How did they know this? How could they have found out? The flood of self-belief she had just experienced faltered and waned. Was Leila right? Had her father been right all those years ago? She did not look at Daniel – she could not.

'I'm sorry,' Leo was saying, as if he genuinely was. 'But I couldn't let you come here to Blue Waters without doing my research.'

Daniel spoke with quiet menace. 'We are here by your invitation and we have done exactly as you wished. We have fulfilled our part of the bargain. If you are unhappy with the result, then there is nothing more to say. We will leave now – after you have paid us our fee.'

Leila reared up, her eyes blazing with triumph. 'Fee? The police would be very interested to learn just what you're up to these days, Mr Roxburgh. My friends in the force tell me they have quite a file on you.'

Far away a door slammed.

'I have been here before,' Evie said dully, as if she were trying to convince herself as much as Leila. 'I remember. They're not fantasies, and I'm not mad.'

Leila sniffed in disgust, but Leo smiled. 'I'm sorry you have these delusions,' he said. 'It must be very difficult for you. But we cannot help you. Perhaps you need to find professional treatment?'

They really were trying to make out she was mad. For a moment the doubts held her down. They were drowning her. But Evie was stronger than that; she'd had to be. The blue was real, she reminded herself, not a delusion. She had been here before. She felt it and knew it. And most importantly of all, she saw it in their eyes.

'I was here!' Her gaze swept over them all – Raymond and Diana standing close, faces slack with shock, Leo watching as though he were an observer rather than a participant, and Leila, her anger hardly contained.

The fragments of memory rolled over her, each one in itself stark and clear and all slotting together to make a whole. There were still gaps, far too many of them, but enough of the picture was coming together for her to believe that she was right.

That was when the word she had been searching for came back to her. The word that the cold breath had whispered into her ear. The French-woman's name.

'Genevieve,' she said.

Leila's pale face blazed, and froze. There was a pause, no one dared speak and then she said in a harsh, bitter voice, 'Pay them, Leo.'

'But, Mother −' Puzzled, he looked from one to the other. 'I thought we agreed that −'

'Pay them. Get them out of here. I want them gone.'

CHAPTER 10

❦

THE LIGHTS OF BLUE WATERS were receding behind them. The clamour in Evie's head was easing and shifting again into that cold, false tranquillity that had seen her through many an anxious moment in her life.

But there was a new picture in her head now. An image of a child squeezed into a cupboard in a mahogany sideboard on the upper landing. Her tiny body was very still and she was barely breathing.

Hide, hide, urged Genevieve's voice in her head. *Do not move, Evangeline.*

So she didn't. She stayed hidden, a cold little bundle, until long after darkness. But Genevieve never returned.

'Evie?' It was Daniel, glancing at her anxiously as he drove. 'How are you feeling?'

Behind them, in the rear view mirror, Blue Waters had vanished from sight. A few scattered lights shone out on their right, while, to their left, lay the blank vastness of the bay. They were going home, but the thought didn't bring her any joy.

'Do you believe I'm mad?' she asked. 'You heard what Leila said.'

Daniel shot her a longer look — and she felt his eyes on her in the darkness. He began to slow the car down, and then pulled over onto the side of the road, the tyres crunching on the gravel. There was probably a very nice view to the bay, but Evie couldn't see it. A single light flickered out over the dark water and she could hear the waves washing onto the shore.

'Tell me,' he said, just a voice in the dark. 'No more secrets.'

He was right, the time for secrets was over. It seemed as good a moment as any to finally tell him her story.

'I ran away from my father when I was fourteen. My mother and I, we both ran away. We took a suitcase with just a few things in it, not many. We couldn't carry much.'

'Why did you run away?' He growled the words.

He was angry, she thought, and she was surprised. Well, that was good, wasn't it? Better anger than pity, or rejection.

'The Frenchwoman, that was why.'

'The Frenchwoman,' he murmured, bemused.

'Yes. I started to hear the Frenchwoman in my dreams and then I started to speak her words. She was inside my head, somehow. When my father heard me he was furious and terrified of me, all at the same time. Leila was right, though I didn't know it then. I think he was going to send me away to be locked up. And my mother knew it. After he heard me speaking the Frenchwoman's words, she was so afraid. All that week she crept about as if she had some awful burden on her shoulders. I suppose that was it. And then he had to work late, and that was her chance. She and I ran. We hid ourselves away in a little country town, changed our names, pretended to be other people. But she never really believed she was safe. Even when she was dying, she worried about me being found.'

'And yet you came back here.'

'I did. I even changed my name back again. I thought I deserved it. I was a grown woman and I didn't have to be afraid of my father any more. My mother was frightened all her life, Daniel, and I swore I was never going to be like that.'

He took a cigarette out of his case and lit it, half opening the window to get rid of the smoke. He was smiling. 'So you're a hero.'

The old joke. Evie managed a shaky laugh. 'I am, aren't I? Or too bloody stupid for words. I thought I only had my father to worry about, but now I'm beginning to think there was far more to it than that.' She swallowed. 'The Frenchwoman is the key to it. Now do you see why I didn't want to play-act any more? She had found me, and every time I played my part she grew stronger. I thought it was happening to me all over again, just as it did when I was fourteen. I thought I was losing my mind and I simply wanted it to stop.'

'Genevieve,' Daniel said. 'Is that her name?'

'Yes.' Evie felt herself smile. *Genevieve.* The Frenchwoman had a name after all these years, and now Evie was wondering why it had taken her so long to remember it.

'Leila recognised the name.' He was thinking; she could almost hear his mind ticking over. 'That was why she caved in at the last moment and had Leo pay us. You realise that, don't you?'

'Yes. When I was a child my father locked me up – punishment, he called it – for lying. He said my memories were lies and I had to learn to stop lying. I didn't stop remembering; I just stopped telling him about them. I suppose that was his job, to keep the secret.'

The secret of Genevieve and her death.

'Evie,' he groaned. 'Christ, Evie.' He sounded as if he were in more pain than she was.

'But now I know the truth and it was the blue window that showed me. That window at Blue Waters. I've always seen the blue in my head, but I didn't think it really existed. But it does. It's not imagined; it's a memory. And this afternoon, when I was standing on the landing in front of the blue window, I remembered.'

'Remembered what, though?' he whispered.

'Myself as a child. Hiding. In 1908. Genevieve was there and she told me to hide – so I did. Only she never came back for me. They found me – or I crawled out. Leila made me stand before her and tell them what I had seen, but I shook my head and wouldn't speak. I was so brave.' She laughed with a sound that was almost a sob. 'She said to me, *You're a proper little lady, aren't you?* I've remembered that all my life, and then suddenly just now, in the sitting room, the words came back to me in Leila's voice, and I knew. I knew. I can't tell you how wonderful it is to finally *know*, Daniel.'

He'd gone quiet. The waves lapped down on the shore, and Evie felt as if she had all the time in the world. There was a sense of peace inside her that had never been there before – of acceptance for what she was and relief for what she wasn't.

'I think you're right,' he said and he paused to draw on his cigarette. 'I think you've been to Blue Waters before. It's the only explanation. Leila believes it. She doesn't want you to remember. She was willing to threaten us and then pay us off to stop us from going any further with this thing.'

Her voice was hushed in the darkness, the words precious. 'Genevieve was a real person. A woman who lived and died. And I think she died there, in Blue Waters. I think that's why Leila was so angry and afraid.'

'She's been protecting Henry all her life,' Daniel agreed. 'And she's still doing it. The ruby you described around Genevieve's neck, the dirty dress and torn hands. Did Henry take her as another of his mistresses, only to murder her later?'

'Leila,' Evie spoke with deep certainty. 'If anyone murdered her, then it was Leila. And when she discovered that I had seen it all, she –'

But what did she do? Tell her father to keep a watch on his daughter and if she ever showed signs of remembering or, worse, speaking about it, lock her up? If it was 1908, then she herself would have been very young, only four years old. Perhaps they thought she would forget it all soon enough and they would be safe. Then Henry's memory would be sanctified once more.

'I've come this far,' she went on, 'and I can't stop now. I have to know the truth.'

His cigarette glowed beside her. 'They won't like that, you know. The Grieves family is still powerful. They have friends and they can pull strings. They could hurt you. Do you really want to take the risk?'

It was dangerous. Leila was not a woman who backed away from a challenge, Evie knew that. She was afraid, of course, but it was too late now to stop. She knew she would never be whole again unless she solved this riddle once and for all.

'So is it revenge you want?' Daniel's quiet voice prodded her. 'Do you want Leila charged and sentenced and hanged? Because if that's what you want then I think you'll be disappointed.'

'I just want to know the truth,' she said with a catch in her voice. 'Is that too much to ask? All my life I've been lied to and hurt and frightened, and now I just want to know *why*.'

'All right,' he murmured, reaching over to brush away the tears she didn't even know she was crying. 'All right, then. Let's find out the truth. The first thing we need to do is to prove you were inside Blue Waters all those years ago. How old do you think you were again?'

She moved back, embarrassed, and wiped her face with her sleeve. 'Four. Old enough to assimilate what was happening but young enough not to understand it properly.'

'Tell me about your father,' he said, and his mind was working, scheming. Daniel Roxburgh was doing what he did best.

'He was a valet. A gentleman's gentleman. Oh!'

Why hadn't she ever realised it before? Her father was a servant, her mother a seamstress. They worked in and around the wealthy houses of Melbourne. They would know of Blue Waters. They might even have worked for the Grieves family at some point.

'It makes perfect sense,' he said, following her train of thought. 'Where is he now?'

'I don't know. He could be anywhere. He could be dead.'

'I'll find out.' He started the car. 'Leave it to me for now.'

Evie looked at him. She realised that she trusted him, she believed in him, and that maybe she was even beginning to love him. Perhaps she and Daniel did have a future after all, when all this was over. Or were the problems they faced too big even for Daniel Roxburgh?

Earle Street hadn't changed. Evie felt as if it should have, because *she* had changed. She had been through hell and yet despite it all there was a centre of stillness within her. Not only that; there was a small acorn of hope.

Gwen was still up. She was sitting at the kitchen table with her hands resting in front of her, but for once she wasn't knitting. When Evie said her name, she didn't look up, but her shoulders stiffened and her fingers pressed down hard on the scrubbed pine.

'I know,' she said harshly and nodded in the direction of an open newspaper carefully laid out to face the door. It was a copy of the *Melbourne Clarion,* the one paper Evie knew Gwen never took.

Gwen had been sitting there waiting for her, she

realised. With a stab of mingled anxiety and relief, she knew that the lies were over.

She skimmed the newsprint and found the paragraph, about halfway down.

Roxburgh Psychic Agency

Daniel Roxburgh is a detective, but he doesn't go after the living. Mr Roxburgh seeks out the dead and with the help of his beautiful psychic assistant, Miss Evangeline Woodward, he finds them . . .

'Why didn't you tell me the truth?' demanded Gwen. 'You know I can't abide liars. All those times I thought you were out with Dolly, and you were really with *him.*'

Evie found it difficult to meet Gwen's eyes. There was so much pain in them. She had thought about this scene and it was worse than she had expected.

'There wasn't any Dolly, was there? That was a lie, too.'

'No, there wasn't any Dolly.'

Gwen's fingers squeezed into fists. 'Vi came waltzing in here today with that newspaper. "Didn't know me and your Evie was in the same business," she said to me, with a little smile on her face. I felt like a fool and she knew it. She always said you were using me, but I told her you were a good girl. How can I ever hold my head up in Earle Street again?'

'I'm so sorry. Gwen, I didn't tell you because of the way you felt about Daniel. I knew that you —'

'I don't know how you can even think of working for that man.' Her mouth was hard and straight and unforgiving. 'It's his fault that Billy's dead. I couldn't even look at him, I couldn't!'

'Gwen, please don't. Daniel isn't bad. He wouldn't

hurt any of us. You know that.'

'Daniel killed Billy!'

It was useless. Her eyes were red from crying, or trying not to cry, her fingers gnarled and clawed with the arthritis. Evie didn't know what to say to her, but even if she tried to talk about Billy's debts Gwen wouldn't believe her. It had been a very long day and suddenly she just wanted it to be over.

'I'm tired. We'll talk about it in the morning.'

'I bet you're tired,' Gwen hissed. 'I'll bet you are.' And then closed her lips tight, as if to keep her own nasty fears from spilling out.

'Daniel has been paying me to work for him,' Evie said, trying to be calm and reasonable, when her mind and body were numb with guilt and exhaustion. 'The money is good. You know it's good, Gwen, and you know how much we need it. I've been saving up to get us out of here.'

Gwen had been about to launch into another attack, but stopped mid-breath. 'What – out of my Billy's house? You'd like that, wouldn't you? I'll bet you would! Wouldn't want to stay here and be reminded of him, would you? Or maybe you haven't even got that much heart. Maybe you never loved Billy after all!'

Evie turned and walked out of the room.

It was no use. Gwen had wound herself up so tight there was no stopping her. Her hurt and anger were overwhelming and Evie could argue and promise as much as she liked, but Gwen would not see reason tonight, and would probably never forgive her. It all seemed hopeless as Evie dragged herself up the stairs.

Gwen's voice followed her. 'My Billy thought the world of you!'

'He had a funny way of showing it,' Evie muttered, and then felt instantly ashamed.

Behind her, Gwen's accusations grew more cruel and bitter, her tone more anguished. Evie knew that she was feeling as if she had lost Billy all over again, but there didn't seem much point in trying to comfort her.

Upstairs Jimmy was asleep in his cot, his thumb in his mouth and his dark lashes perfect half moons. The sweet innocence of his face soothed her. She brushed a finger over his cheek, enjoying the perfection of his skin. Whatever happened next, whatever Gwen accused her of, she knew that she had done the best she could in the circumstances. She had cared for Jimmy and his grandmother, and would continue to do so. If Gwen let her. Evie had never had a family until she came to Earle Street, and she wasn't about to let it go now without a fight.

The thought was comforting.

She yawned, undressed and slipped into bed. Rain began to fall on the roof and lull her into sleep.

You're a proper little lady, aren't you?

Leila's voice, full of malice. For a moment Evie struggled to remember the exact time and place. A room, lamplight, those pale eyes looking down on her. And little Evie tired and aching, frightened and sad.

The scene began to unfurl before her and she hardly dared breathe in case it stopped.

She won't say anything, madam. Her father stood tall

and stern with his hand heavy on her head. I will see to it.

Leila's eye was fixed on Evie. *I hope so, Frederick,* she said.

Evie's eyes flickered.

I won't tell. She heard a frightened little girl's voice and it was her own. *Cross my heart, Mrs Grieves, and hope to die . . .*

But someone else was there. She felt him close by and yet she was afraid to turn and look. The same man who had taken Genevieve away. She knew it and he knew she did. And standing here with that man and keeping from screaming out at him was more terrifying than anything else – even more frightening than anything Leila Grieves and her father could say.

Was the man Henry?

A shadow at the edge of her vision, he was a little behind her. Evie tried to see him from the corner of her eye. She could make out a three-piece suit and polished brown shoes, but his face eluded her.

The moment was slipping out of her grasp. And then the blue came down upon her and swallowed her up and it was gone. She was back in her bed at number 5 Earle Street, with the rain falling on the roof.

CHAPTER 11

'WE NEED TO SPEAK TO your father.'
Daniel leaned back against the edge of his desk and folded his arms. He looked down his nose at Evie, seated on the sofa in front of him. It was morning, two days later, and she had taken the tram to Little Lonsdale Street and brought Jimmy with her. Gwen was still keeping to her room like a lady in Victorian times and only coming out when Evie wasn't there. Before she left this morning Evie had knocked and asked if Gwen wanted anything, but she hadn't answered.

Things at number 5 were not improving.

Daniel had not long been awake; his hair was still rumpled, his shirt sleeves rolled up to his elbows and the buttons undone at his throat. But despite his sleepy eyes, he looked refreshed and his smile was full of confidence.

A warm tingle ran through her. It felt right to be here with him, no matter what Gwen thought.

'He's living at the Greenleighs Lodging House.'

Evie blinked in amazement and Daniel laughed. 'Your father, Evie. He's at Greenleighs.'

'How do you –'

'Checked it at the post office. Greenleighs is a pretty exclusive sort of place – not cheap. He's been there for two years now. Mr Frederick Woodward is being very well looked after, thank you.'

'Compared with you and Billy, I never went without, Daniel. Perhaps my father was able to save for his old age; perhaps he could afford to move into Greenleighs for his retirement.'

Daniel didn't seem convinced. 'Perhaps. That's something we'll have to ask him.'

Ask him . . . Even though Evie knew it was what she had to do, the idea of seeing her father again was making her feel sick in the stomach. The last time they had been face to face was when she was fourteen. He had been on his way out of the door, all spruced up, and he had paused on the doorstep to look back at her.

You deserve everything you get.

Something in the way he had said it and the distance in his cold eyes made her think that he had not expected to see her again. Not because she was going to run away; he wouldn't have known about that. No, there had been some other plan afoot, which Evie knew nothing of, but her mother suspected.

Her father. She still thought of him as the man he had been then: tall, stern and unapproachable. A stranger in a bowler hat who disliked her, though she didn't understand why.

'I don't think I can,' she burst out.

'Don't lose that stiff upper lip just yet, all right? We need to do this. *You* need to.'

'What if –'

'That's why we're going to visit your father, to see if we can answer some of the 'what ifs'.'

Daniel nodded across at Jimmy, where the little boy was seated on the floor, busy tearing up some sheets of the Roxburgh Agency letterhead. 'Do it for Jimmy's sake,' he said. 'One day he'll want to know.'

Evie felt the familiar wave of fear and dread building inside her, but this time, instead of fighting, she accepted it. She let herself go. The wave might take her into calmer waters, or it might pound her onto the rocks, but whatever happened she knew she had to take the risk. She could not go on as she was for another minute – let alone another year.

'So will you come with me? When I go to see my father? Will you come?'

She knew now she could do it on her own if she had to. She was far stronger than she had ever realised, but it would be so much better if Daniel was with her.

'Of course I'll come,' he said. 'Don't I always?'

He was smiling at her, as if he could see right inside her and as if he liked what he saw.

Jimmy let out a wail, holding up his hand and his bottom lip wobbling. Daniel stooped over him to inspect the cut. 'You'll live,' he said and ruffled the boy's hair. A big tear rolled down Jimmy's cheek.

'Your Uncle Daniel isn't very sympathetic, is he?' Evie said, reaching for her son. 'When do you want to go?' she asked Daniel. 'To Greenleighs?'

He was watching her. 'No time like the present. Just let me get washed and changed.'

'I'm not going to run away, you know,' Evie said.

He smiled. 'I know,' he said gently. 'You're a hero.'

She laughed and buried her face in Jimmy's neck. 'I hope so, Daniel, I really do.'

❦

The Greenleighs Lodging House was set back from the road with a nice garden, mostly roses, dotted with chairs and benches that would be well tenanted on warmer days. Today the hot weather had given way to clouds and a cool breeze, so none of Greenleighs occupants were taking advantage of the outdoors at the moment.

They soon found the office and Daniel gave Mrs Sharpe, the middle-aged woman in charge, his best smile. She melted.

'Mr Woodward is in room 14. He has so few visitors.'

'Well, this is his lucky day. Mrs Rose is Mr Woodward's daughter and this is his grandson, Jimmy.'

Mrs Sharpe glanced over at Evie and Jimmy. 'Oh, how lovely,' she said politely. 'I'm sure he will be pleased to see them. I'll just send someone to fetch him down to the visitors' lounge.'

'Do you mind if we go up and surprise him?' Daniel leaned closer, as if this was a secret just between the two of them.

'Oh, I don't know . . .'

But Mrs Sharpe soon overcame her doubts under his gentle persuasion and directed them up the stairs. 'Room 14 is on the first floor, at the back. Mr Woodward prefers it,' she explained, 'because it is so much quieter. He's a real gentleman, isn't he?' This last was spoken with a degree of awe.

Evie smiled back but she knew it didn't look right. She was about to be reunited with the man who had tormented, threatened her and conspired to have her locked up. What father would do that to his child? She could not believe Billy would be capable of it, or Daniel.

As a child Evie had always secretly believed that his actions were brought on by her own behaviour, that she wasn't good enough. Now when she remembered his frightened face the night he came to her room and overheard her nightmares, she knew that it had nothing to do with how good she was. Frederick Woodward had been prepared to send her away because she was beginning to remember Genevieve, and he had been instructed never to let that happen.

'Evie?' Daniel had found room 14 and had his fist raised waiting to knock. 'Are you ready?'

How could she ever be ready? But she took a deep breath and nodded.

There were footsteps inside the room and the door was thrown open with an authority that sent her spinning back into the past. The sickness in her stomach lurched into her throat. Jimmy squeaked anxiously as she squeezed him too tightly and his protest drew her father's blue eyes from Daniel to herself.

If she was shocked to see him, he was far more shocked to see her. She had not given any thought to the way he would feel; she had only worried about herself. But now she realised that of course he would be surprised. He had probably thought her gone forever. To see her now, standing at his door, would be like coming face to face with the dead.

'Evie?' He mouthed the name as if he wasn't quite sure, and actually staggered, then clung to the door frame.

He had always been old, but now she saw that he was far older than she had remembered. His face was grey and deeply lined and his hair was almost white. Where was the ogre of her childhood?

Strangely, the sight of his emotions helped to calm her own. She had been imagining her father as some terrifying monster, a creature less than human, but now she realised that he was just a man after all – an old one with unhappiness etched sharply into his face. What could she be afraid of here?

'Father.' The odd formality of their relationship struck her anew. Not Papa; never Daddy. They may as well have been strangers. How could she hate someone she had never even known?

'Mr Woodward.' Daniel was the one in control. He steered her father back into his room, his hand firm on the older man's arm, and her father was so shaken that he allowed it, even though Evie remembered how much he had always hated to be touched.

His room was larger than she had imagined, although he had filled it up with furniture from home. Large, heavy pieces she recalled vaguely and that had no place here, but probably reminded him of his glorious past service. A bowler hat, brushed clean and made shiny with wear, rested on a side table, with a walking stick propped beside it. As long as she had known him, her father had worn his bowler hat and carried his walking stick, just like a proper gentleman.

There were, she couldn't help but notice, no photographs: none of herself or her mother tucked away on the bookshelf, no reminders of his family. He was alone, just as he had always wanted to be.

Daniel had closed the door and was standing next to it.

Her father recognised the unspoken threat. 'What do you want?' His voice was shaking, angry, but Evie thought the anger might have been manufactured to hide what he really felt. Fright. Frederick Woodward was afraid. 'You have no right to be here.'

'Father —'

'Evie's come to ask you some questions, Mr Woodward. I hope you'll help her to answer them.'

Her father's wild eyes flicked from Evie and down to Jimmy. If she had hoped for some slight softening in him at the sight of his grandson then she would be disappointed. Frederick winced and looked resolutely back to Daniel.

'I have nothing to say to her,' he said firmly. 'She ran away with my wife, Amy. All ties between us were severed at that point.'

Daniel's expression didn't change, but Evie read the fury in the sudden tensing of his shoulders. He was a dangerous man, she knew that, and she thought by the way her father was watching him that *he* could see it too.

'Evie has had some disturbing dreams, Mr Woodward,' Daniel said, in his quiet, level voice, as if they were friends, just having a chat. 'Perhaps you can help her understand what they're all about.'

Her father's face turned even greyer than before

and the lines about his mouth deepened. He seemed to be struggling to catch his breath.

'She was always having dreams. Insanity runs in Amy's – in her mother's family. That was why we were so worried about her.'

'That's a lie!' Evie hissed.

Frederick did not answer her, but stared at Daniel, daring him to contradict his statement.

But Daniel didn't suffer from the same paralysing doubts as Evie. He took a step towards Frederick and although they were around the same height, Daniel was younger. He looked bigger, stronger and far more intimidating.

'Is that really the truth, Mr Woodward? I think you were worried about her because of her dreams. I think you were worried because of the Frenchwoman. Genevieve.'

His mouth opened and closed, but no sound came out. The name had shocked him. Or maybe he saw something in Daniel's eyes that Evie couldn't.

She had never known her father to be frightened, or seen him vulnerable. Until now she had not believed he could be.

Daniel kept on speaking. 'When Evie was a child, did she ever go to Blue Waters, Mr Woodward? Blue Waters – it's a mansion on the bay. Sir Henry Grieves built it. Now, think carefully before you answer, because this time I want the truth.'

Frederick shot a look sideways at Evie, then down at the floor. His face was stiff and his mouth hardly opened when he answered. 'You don't know what you're asking.'

'Yes, I do. I'm asking for the truth.'

He shook his head stubbornly, back and forth,

like Jimmy did when he found Daniel's letter opener and didn't want to give it up.

'Father, please!'

Frederick glanced at her again and this time it was long enough for her to see exactly what was in his eyes. Hatred, loathing. He was wishing she had never found him.

Frozen to the spot, Evie could only watch as Daniel bent towards the older man and murmured something in his ear. Frederick jerked back.

'Who are you?' his voice quavered.

'Daniel Roxburgh. I'm Evie's friend, Mr Woodward. Just you remember it.'

'You can't speak to me like that –'

'I don't make idle threats,' Daniel cut him short, 'and I can speak to you any way I like. Now, tell us what we want to know and we'll leave you alone.'

Frederick glared at him a moment more, but it was only bravado. He believed now that Daniel meant what he said and his past and the people in it could not save him.

'Very well,' he said it with resentment. 'The truth is that I was Sir Henry Grieves's valet, his manservant. Your mother was a seamstress who used to come in for work. She was never good enough with the needle to suit Mrs Grieves, however, and after we married she gave it up.'

It was true then. Both were servants to the Grieves family and loyal to Sir Henry and Leila.

'I was there, wasn't I?' Evie asked, the excitement making her tremble. 'I was at Blue Waters?'

But her father ignored her and poked a bony finger at Daniel's chest, although not quite daring to make contact. 'I have important friends. Don't make the mistake of thinking I'm all alone in the world. I'll see you dealt with. Taught a lesson by your betters, sir!'

Daniel grinned. 'I wouldn't count on it,' he drawled. 'My friends own bigger guns. But if you want to start a war – ?'

Even Frederick Woodward, gentleman's gentleman, knew when to back down.

'You don't know what you're getting yourselves into,' he blustered. 'It all happened so long ago. Can't you forget it and let sleeping dogs lie?'

Was that a plea in his eyes? Evie wanted to believe it was from a wish to see her safe from danger, but in her heart she doubted his concern was for her. More likely he was worried about himself, his nice room and the consequences when whoever was paying for it found out that Daniel and she had paid him a visit.

'I can't forget it,' she said woodenly. 'I'll never be able to until I know the truth. Until I know about Genevieve.'

'I made a promise twenty years ago.' His breathing was getting shorter and more laboured. He looked awful. 'I promised Leila Grieves,' he wheezed.

Daniel reached out for a chair and, guiding the old man's arm, lowered him onto it. Frederick sat stiffly, unprotesting, but unswayed, too.

'We were at Blue Waters yesterday,' Evie said and watched as he turned to her, his eyes wide and shocked. 'I met Leila and Leo and Raymond. But at no stage did they tell me that they had met me before. Why was that, do you think?'

He laughed with a sound like rustling leaves.

'Was Genevieve one of Sir Henry's women?

Can't you tell me that, at least? Did my mother take me there and then leave me? Why didn't anyone notice I was gone? How could I have been hidden inside that place and no one knew?'

He was defiant.

Evie felt like hitting him, but she knew she wouldn't, or couldn't. 'Evie?' Daniel was watching her. He jerked his head at Frederick and quirked an eyebrow. He wanted to know whether he should force her father to answer.

She looked at the old man, seated upright in his chair, clearly ill, but determined to be stubborn to the last. His misdirected loyalties had caused her a great deal of misery, but she wasn't going to add to them by resorting to violence. Or by asking Daniel to do it for her.

'Let's go,' she said and moved towards the door. But once there she remembered something she had forgotten and turned around again. Her father was staring at her suspiciously.

'You're wasting your time,' he said.

'Oh, I know that,' she retorted. 'You'd prefer to give your life to an old man who didn't care a jot about you or anyone else. Even his own sons hate him. No, you keep your loyalty, Father. I don't want it. All I was going to tell you was your grandson's name. Just in case you ever want to know.' Her voice softened. 'He's called Jimmy.'

He looked surprised and then his mouth pinched up. He didn't care; it meant nothing to him. Evie knew then that she would never see him again, but she was glad she had come this time. At least now she knew he was no monster. Frederick Woodward would never give her nightmares again.

'They were going to have you disposed of, you know,' he said suddenly. 'That night when you and Amy ran away. They were coming for you. She must have known it.'

'Disposed of?' she whispered, not wanting to believe that he meant what she thought he did. 'You mean locked up somewhere?'

Frederick pursed his lips. 'What would be the point of that? You'd talk and questions would be asked. No, they were going to take you out onto the bay and throw you overboard.'

You deserve everything you get . . .

'It was your own fault,' he went on. 'You wouldn't stop talking about it. You wouldn't just forget it. So you brought it on yourself.'

And he really believed it. She could see that in his eyes.

'I was fourteen,' she said. 'I was a child and I needed to hear the truth. Maybe then I could have forgotten it. Instead, I was punished for reasons I didn't understand. I relived what had happened to me over and over again, when you locked me in the kitchen cupboard. You stupid, ignorant man! This is all your fault.'

'Evie,' Daniel took her arm. She was shaking so hard she could hardly walk. Jimmy wailed and Daniel took him from her, holding him with one arm and steering her with the other. He turned at the door and gave Frederick a look over his shoulder. 'I'll be coming for you,' he said.

They left room 14 and went back down the stairs.

Mrs Sharpe was waiting in her office and came out when she heard them, all smiles. Her face clouded a little when she saw Evie's expression, but Daniel assured her that all had gone well and thanked her again for her help.

'Mr Woodward isn't always the easiest of guests,' she admitted. 'I didn't even realise he had any family living. It certainly doesn't say so on his file.'

'His file?' Daniel turned to Evie. 'Why don't you take Jimmy out to the car,' he said. 'I need to check something here before we go.'

When he joined her in the Oldsmobile, he was wearing a grim smile and there was a glitter of excitement in his eyes. 'Listen. I saw your father's file. I told Mrs Sharpe that you wanted to do your bit to help him, financially, and that you didn't understand how he could afford to stay in a place like Greenleighs.'

'Daniel —' she pulled away irritably.

'No, wait. Listen to me. It's as I thought. Someone else is paying the bills.'

Evie stared back at him. 'But who?'

'Grieves. No first name. The money comes out of a special trust fund set up by them for your father. It makes perfect sense, Evie. Your father's kept his mouth shut all these years and he's been well paid for it.'

'Genevieve was murdered. And my father knew about it and helped cover it up.'

'Yes, I think so.'

'And I was there. I saw something. And when I started to remember, they were going to murder me, too. The nightmares were getting me noticed. People were asking questions. And they couldn't have had that.'

Bleak as it was, Evie faced the truth.

'I think you know what happened at Blue Waters.

I think the whole thing is there, inside your head. The nightmares were part of remembering. The Frenchwoman was part of it.'

She shuddered. He was right. Somewhere in her past were all the answers, but they were fragmented. The memories of a very frightened child.

'Leila must have been beside herself when Leo told her about me,' she said slowly. 'Evangeline Woodward. It's an unusual name. She would have needed to see me and judge for herself whether or not I was still a danger to the family.'

'You'd already seen Genevieve then,' Daniel reminded her. 'At Muriel Nelson's. Leo was there and he heard you. He would have told Leila about it. And then at the Beatsons' it happened again. Leila would have heard about that, too.'

Evie turned to him. 'Yes, of course! She was checking up on me.'

No wonder Leila had been so defensive. She was still protecting Henry after all these years.

'I have to know the truth,' she said now. 'I have to know who killed Genevieve and why I was there, and why they are still pretending she didn't exist. I've come too far now to stop, Daniel.'

'I don't want you to stop,' he assured her and his hand was warm as he laid it on hers. 'Keep digging, Evie. Eventually we're going to find Genevieve.'

She swallowed. 'Yes,' she said. 'Or her bones.'

Gwen had come out of her room by the time Evie returned to Earle Street. She was still withdrawn and wounded and Evie admitted she had every right to feel that way. But she took hope from the glint of relief in the older woman's eyes, when she saw Evie come through the door carrying Jimmy.

Perhaps Gwen had begun to convince herself that Evie had gone for good and taken her grandson with her. Evie was sure that eventually Gwen would be able to forgive her – perhaps not to the extent of allowing Daniel into their lives, not straightaway, but for Jimmy's sake Gwen would agree to move from Earle Street. And at least that was something.

'I went to see my father,' Evie explained, although Gwen hadn't asked. 'I haven't seen him for ten years. I thought I hated him and maybe I do. I used to be so frightened of him and everything to do with him, but looking at him today – I'm not frightened anymore, Gwen. And I don't think he'll ever frighten me again. What he is is so far removed from what I am that I can't even believe he's my father any more.'

Gwen didn't reply, but studiously ignored her.

With a sigh, Evie carried Jimmy up to her room. The little boy had fallen asleep in Daniel's car and now she laid him gently in his cot and tucked the blanket around him.

'Evie?'

When she turned around, Gwen was standing in the doorway, her arms folded across her chest. She looked as if she might scream, or cry, or both.

'Gwen?' Evie moved towards her.

But Gwen's voice came out in a rush. 'Promise me you won't leave me! I lost Billy, I couldn't bear it if I lost you and Jimmy, too!'

Relieved, Evie wrapped her arms tight about her. Here was her real family; not that sad old man clinging to the loyalties of the past.

'I'm not going anywhere,' she said. 'Not without you, anyway. But I do want us to leave Earle Street, Gwen. We can do better than this. I want to see Jimmy grow up somewhere safe, with proper gardens, where he can play outside without me worrying that he might get hurt.'

Gwen nodded, clinging. 'I know, I know. Sometimes it's hard, that's all. I think about Billy and if we go from here it'll be like leaving a part of him behind.'

'We could never leave Billy behind. He'd always be with us, I promise you that.'

After a moment Gwen wiped her eyes. 'I don't like Daniel,' she grumbled. 'I can't help what I feel.'

Evie half-smiled. 'I really don't care whether you like Daniel or not, you know. I like him. And Jimmy likes him. He's looked after us in ways you don't even know about. He's not perfect, but then neither am I. Or you. Give him a chance, that's all. Remember how grateful Billy would have been that Daniel – his best mate – is here now, standing in for him.'

Gwen bit back the retort that was burning her lips.

'Besides, Daniel has plans. He's going to Perth.'

'Aren't you going with him?' Gwen asked, the worry deepening the lines on her face again and her eyes starting to water.

'How can I?' Evie scolded. 'I have you and Jimmy to look after.'

'Oh.' Gwen tried not to look so pleased about it, but unlike Evie she wasn't good at hiding her feelings. 'That's a shame then,' she added for good measure. Her eye sharpened. 'What was that you were saying about your father, Evie?'

'Nothing. He doesn't matter.'

And with a sense of relief, she realised it was true. Apart from the secrets he held, her father was unimportant. His power over her had finally gone.

CHAPTER 12

E VIE HAD SPENT A MORNING looking at houses. By the time she returned to Earle Street she felt as though she had narrowed it down to one in particular, large enough for Gwen and Jimmy and herself, but not overwhelming. And the neighbourhood was pleasant.

The gangly lad was on the corner, watching her go past, but as usual she ignored him. It wasn't until she reached number 5 that she saw the car: a big white one, with a driver waiting beside it, smoking discreetly.

She hurried inside.

Gwen looked up from the teapot, her eyes glazed and her expression hovering somewhere between pleasure and shell-shock. 'Evie! It's Diana Ashman. The actress!'

Evie could see that it was. Diana, elegant in a *crepe de chine* dress and matching cloche hat, gave her a bright, professional and completely sober smile. 'Evie! I'm so sorry to be a nuisance, but I did so want to see you again and Gwen was kind enough to let me wait.'

'You're not a nuisance,' Gwen scolded. 'How could you think that? I was just saying, Evie, how much I loved Miss Ashman in "Bushland Lady". I saw that film three times, I'm sure I did.'

Diana smiled and thanked her, but didn't take her eyes from Evie. There was a message in the way she looked at her or maybe a plea to be heard. Evie sat down carefully, wondering what it was that Diana had come to say.

Gwen rambled on about pictures in general and Diana spoke about the new one Raymond was filming. She was polite, but Evie was sure she was only waiting her chance. It came when Jimmy woke, his wails quickly growing louder and more desperate.

Gwen looked to Evie to deal with him, but Diana turned to her with a broad smile and a 'Would you mind, Mrs Rose? I just wanted to have a word with Evie on a private matter. You understand, don't you?'

Gwen looked puzzled and then her brow cleared. 'Oh, you want a *reading*! Why didn't you say so.' And she bustled off to tend to Jimmy.

'I know you don't want a reading,' Evie said, when Diana didn't immediately start to speak. 'So what have you come here for? You'd better tell me quickly. She'll be back in a moment.'

Diana waved her hand. 'I felt I should apologise for what happened that weekend at Blue Waters. It was nasty. I've thought about it quite a lot since.'

Evie just waited.

Diana laughed nervously. 'The Grieves are a close-knit family, I think you've gathered that; they don't tell tales about each other. Leila is very protective of Sir Henry's memory, still. There was so much scandal and gossip while he was alive and Leila seems determined to sanctify him now he's dead.'

Evie looked her directly in the eye. 'Did you know about Genevieve before I mentioned her?'

'You don't hedge about, do you, Evie? I had heard of her, yes. I overheard Leila once, but it just sounded like another scandal that she had had to hush it up. I thought she must have paid Genevieve to keep her mouth shut; she did that often while Henry was alive. And as he got older he got worse. No woman was safe from him.'

'Was Genevieve a servant?'

Diana shrugged. 'I don't know.' Her fingers trembled as she lit another cigarette. 'Do you think she's dead? Is that it? Genevieve's spirit is telling you that she is dead and my husband's family had something to do with it?'

Evie didn't answer her.

'Murder is a rather serious allegation,' Diana sighed. 'You had best be very careful before you start accusing anybody of something like that. How do you know this Genevieve didn't just run off? Or get paid off?'

'She told me.'

Diana's smile was uncertain at the edges. 'I see.' She nodded, and drew on her cigarette. She looked around as if she'd like a drink, but Gwen had only a bottle of cooking sherry and that was hidden deep in the cupboard.

'You and Leo are having an affair, aren't you?'

'It's no secret. He's very charming. Irresistible, in fact. Rather like your Daniel.'

'I can see that he would be. That genial, eager-
to-please manner is very appealing. Like a little boy
who hasn't quite grown up.'

'Yes.' Diana flicked some ash from her dress. 'I
fell in love with him. Unfortunately so did Honora, and Leo has been alternating between us. Like
father, like son.'

'I'm sorry.'

'Why should you be? I'm married to Raymond
after all. He's a good man – a little self-obsessed, but
he loves me. He'll take me back. He always does.
It was Leo who suggested I marry Raymond, you
know. Not because he was being kind to either of
us, but because he was trying to hurt his brother
– he does that all the time, in his own subtle way.
He hates him for what he did to his leg all those
years ago. But actually, I've begun to realise that
maybe I got myself the better deal. Raymond is far
nicer than Leo and far more stable. He's promised
me a cruise this time,' she added with just the right
touch of excitement. But it jarred with the misery
in her eyes.

'Leo thinks you're play-acting, you know,' she
said suddenly. 'He believes that Daniel learned
about Genevieve somehow or other and intends
to blackmail Leila into paying him to keep quiet.
I heard him telling her before you arrived that
weekend.'

Evie tried to hide her shock and a new sense of
dread. Leo, the charmer, Leo the liar. 'It has nothing
to do with Daniel,' she said, 'and we're not black-
mailing anybody. I just want to know the truth.'

'Ah, the truth!' Diana stubbed out her cigarette
and stood up. 'If I were you, I'd think quite hard

about how much the truth means to you. Is it worth losing your reputation for? Is it worth losing your life?'

She spoke in an ironic way that was almost joking, but Evie knew she wasn't joking.

Gwen was disappointed to come back and find Diana gone. 'I've never had an actress is my home before,' she said. 'In fact I don't think there's ever been one in the whole of Earle Street. Wait until I tell Vi.'

Evie was wondering what Diana had really wanted. To warn her? Whatever the reason for her visit it had brought with it a new sense of urgency. She felt as if she were standing on that narrow ledge and it was starting to crumble away.

The following morning Evie took Gwen to see the house. Gwen was impressed, speaking at first in a hushed voice she only used in picture theatres and churches. 'Such a nice neighbourhood,' she kept saying, on the way home in the tram. 'All those fences in straight lines and not a single picket missing.'

'What do you think then?' Evie said, jiggling Jimmy on her knee as he began to wriggle. 'Should I put down a deposit?'

Gwen bit her lip. 'I don't know. It's a big decision.'

Evie straightened up in her seat. 'I have the money,' she said.

'You do what you think best, dear. But don't do

it for me, will you? I don't need a picket fence to be happy. As long as I know you and Jimmy are close by, then that's enough for me!'

❦

'She nearly had me in tears,' Evie told Daniel.

She had come around to his office in Little Lonsdale Street, and saw at once the "For Lease" sign in the window. His files were scattered about on the floor and desk. 'I'm sorting them,' he explained. 'Most of them will have to be burned, in case the police ever take an interest.'

'Would they follow you all the way to Perth?'

'They might.'

'You know if you're serious about a new start, then it has to be a proper one.'

'Of course.' He raised his eyebrows, challenging her to doubt him.

'I had a call from Mrs Sharpe,' he added, carefully stacking some files. 'The woman from Greenleighs.'

'Oh?'

'Your father has left. Seems he can no longer afford to pay the fees. She doesn't have a forwarding address, she said. He wouldn't give her one. She seemed upset, so I think he must have been rude to her before he left – but in a gentlemanly way, I'm sure.'

'Does that mean the Grieves family is no longer paying for him to stay silent? Or do you think they suspect he talked?'

'Only he can tell you that, Evie, and he doesn't seem to want to be found.' He stopped fiddling with the files and looked up at her. 'I could find him, if you asked me to. But maybe I'm part of the reason he's gone into hiding.'

She thought about it. Did she want to know where he was? Did it really matter? 'No. I don't need to see him again, and I'm fairly certain he doesn't want to see me. Let's forget him, let him go,' she said.

He grinned. 'You seem much more comfortable with yourself these days. No more bad dreams?'

'Not recently, no. I don't think they're altogether gone. I suspect Genevieve knows we're doing our best to find her, and she's waiting patiently.'

'You frighten me sometimes. When you saw Genevieve at Blue Waters, was she just a memory, or was she a spirit?'

'I don't know. I can't say. Maybe my mind made her into a ghost.'

'I found out which year they closed up the tunnel to the beach. 1908. Leila said it was too dangerous to use and they blocked it off. No one's been down there since.'

Genevieve was down there still, Evie was certain of it.

'How can we ever prove any of this?'

'We can't. We just have to hope one of the Grieves confesses, or makes a mistake.'

'That reminds me, Diana Ashman came to see me.' She went on to tell him what the actress had said.

'Sounds like Leo is a chip off the old block.'

'But I can't believe he would hurt anyone.'

Daniel sat down beside her on the sofa. 'Not even for Leila?' he asked, and reached out and touched her cheek. His fingers were warm and gentle, stroking her skin. Evie felt the slow burn of passion ignite inside her.

When he leaned over and kissed her she didn't stop him. 'Stay a while,' he whispered.

She wanted to. She knew it with a terrible ache in her heart. She turned into his arms and kissed him back. Was there a future for the two of them? Despite what she had said to Gwen about their futures being separate, she hoped so. She would miss him so much when he left.

There was a loud knock on the door.

Daniel got up and went to his desk. Evie felt the smile freeze on her mouth as she watched him reach into the drawer and take out a gun. It was small and fitted neatly into his trouser pocket, hardly making a wrinkle. Of course Daniel would have a gun. He always had one. How could she have forgotten that? She had been thinking of him as an ordinary man, but he wasn't. Life with him was never ordinary.

The unstable feeling inside her was back. *This* was why she had chosen Billy, and why she had never felt safe with Daniel.

He glanced at her now, a warning, before he called for the visitor to come in.

The man she remembered from the other day, the one with the Gladstone bag, came in first. His broad shoulders filled the doorway, and his dark hair was smoothed down with brilliantine. Behind him was another man: smaller, plump but dapper in a grey suit. His brown eyes slid curiously over Evie before turning to Daniel.

She hadn't seen Gunner Connor for a while, but

she knew him instantly. That same smooth unlined face, as if what he did for a living had no effect upon him. He still smiled without opening his mouth because he was ashamed of his teeth. He'd had them fixed, she'd heard, but it was a habit he couldn't seem to break.

Like killing people.

'Gunner.' Daniel sat back on his desk and rested his hands on the edge of it, one either side of his hips. 'I was going to call in and see you.'

Connor looked at the cracked leather sofa and decided to stand. 'I thought I'd save you the trouble,' he said. 'Evie, isn't it? Billy Rose's wife? I heard about Billy. Got a boy, is that right? What's his name?'

'I – it's Jimmy.' She was stammering. She couldn't seem to help herself, even when she saw the twitch of irritation it caused on Connor's face.

'What's wrong?' He all but shouted it at her. 'I don't hurt kids. When have I ever hurt a kid?'

'Evie,' Daniel warned her softly.

Be calm, be calm. It will be all right. She felt like her mother, running from the house with the door swinging open behind her, running to the train station, running all her life. Looking for safety, something so elusive that she never found it and probably wouldn't have recognised it if she did.

Evie knew she didn't want to live like that.

Connor had come around the sofa and now stood in front of Daniel. The broad shouldered man stayed where he was, near the door, his eyes deceptively sleepy.

'I was thinking, Danny,' Connor said jovially, as if he and Daniel were best friends. 'You could do a job for me. There's a bloke in Brunswick needs seeing to. Can't seem to keep his fingers out of my share of a club over there. You could do that for me, Danny. What do you say? It could be the start of a new partnership, eh? Only I'd be the boss, like, and you'd do what I told you to.'

Evie was horrified. Surely Daniel wouldn't agree to something like that? And yet he seemed to be considering it.

'I don't know, Gunner,' he said with feigned reluctance. 'I promised I'd go straight, you see. Fresh start and all that. I can't go back on my word, can I?'

Connor kept smiling, but not with his eyes. 'Come on, Danny, we both know that won't happen! You go straight? You were born to lie crooked in your bed.' He laughed, looking about him as if expecting them all to laugh too. The broad shouldered man snorted, and settled his feet more firmly on the floor.

Daniel shrugged. 'Maybe you're right, Gunner, but I've got to try. I won't know unless I do, will I?'

Connor wasn't laughing now. He looked serious and very dangerous. 'I don't understand you, Danny. I give you this opportunity and you knock me back. We used to be friends, didn't we? Are you saying I'm not good enough for you any more?'

Daniel slid his hand into his pocket. Evie tried not to show what she was thinking, but she felt as if she was about to scream.

'A promise is a promise, Gunner,' he said quietly.

'Who'd you promise?' Connor's eyes narrowed. Evie was sure he was going through a list of all the would-be underworld bosses. He was worried that Daniel would work against him, rather than for him.

Daniel's eyes met Evie's over his head. 'I promised Evie here,' he said. 'She won't have me unless I go straight, Gunner.'

Connor stared at him and then he began to laugh. He doubled over, still laughing. Even his meaty henchman snorted once or twice. At last he caught his breath, shook his head and slapped Daniel on the back.

'Daniel Roxburgh being led along by a girl! I always thought you were a man to look up to, Danny.' His face went hard. 'Where's the money?'

Daniel reached back, found it and handed it to him. Connor weighed it in his hand, then threw it over to his bagman.

'Think about what I said, Danny.' There was a sneer in his voice now, as if Daniel had slipped in his estimation.

'Bye, Gunner.'

There was a long silence when the door closed.

'That was dangerous,' Evie said. She stood up and reached for her purse, her hands trembling.

Daniel got there first, handed it to her and at the same time bent down to kiss her mouth. He was good at kissing. The tension of the last few moments dissolved in passion and maybe it was almost enough. Almost.

She stepped back away from him.

'You were safe,' Daniel promised her. 'I would have put a hole between his eyes before I'd have let him hurt you.'

She shivered. 'I'm glad you didn't. Daniel –'

Something in her face must have alerted him.

He touched her hair, her cheek. 'Don't say it,' he whispered. 'Don't make any decisions now. Please.'

'Will you do as Connor asked?' She looked him straight in the eye and saw him look sideways, just a little, as he told the lie.

'Of course not.'

She turned away, nodding as if she believed him, and felt fragile, as if she might cry. Had she really begun to believe that she and Daniel could be together? They were suited in so many ways, but she knew she could never be with a man who lived the sort of life Gunner Connor did. Who might be out doing things she knew nothing about and hated the thought of. *Like sorting a bloke in Brunswick.*

'I'll take you home, before it starts raining again.'

She looked back at him, standing there in his shirt sleeves, handsome and so sure of himself. And she felt as if she had lost something precious.

'I don't need –'

'Course you do. Don't worry, I won't come in and frighten Gwen. I have to drop round somewhere afterwards. One last thing I have to do. One last appointment and then I'm free of this town.'

What could she say? He was Daniel and she loved him. It wasn't his fault she would never be able to live happily ever after with him.

'Thank you, Daniel. I'd be very glad for you to drive me home.'

*

From habit he parked the Oldsmobile around

the corner from Earle Street. For a moment they sat, silent, and savoured being together.

'What are we going to do?' he said.

'I don't know. I wish I could make Leo talk to me. He might tell me the truth. I doubt Leila will – and Raymond just wants to forget.'

'I didn't mean about Genevieve,' he said. 'I meant about us.'

That was more difficult. 'I told you that Gwen and I went to look at a house.'

'So you'll all live there together, just like at number 5? Keep Billy's memory going? Burn a candle to him every night?'

'Don't –'

'Oh, I know, don't say anything bad about Billy. He was never a saint, Evie. We both know that. If you want a man who'll love you all your life, who'll never let you down, then come with me. I love you, and despite what you say, I think you love me. There's not much happiness in this world so you don't want to throw any of it away.'

'Sometimes you're a stranger to me, Daniel. I don't like surprises. That's why I married Billy, I suppose. I wanted things to be simple, for every day to be the same.'

'Oh Evie, that's sad.' He pulled a face and made her laugh despite herself. 'I think you need a man like me, a man who'll take you out dancing to a different spot every night. Who'll make love to you in the sun and the rain. Maybe sometimes I'll do things you won't like, but it won't be because I want to hurt or worry you. We'll both make mistakes, but that's just part of being together. Life's an adventure, Evie. Come and share it with me.'

'No,' she said. 'You're going to take Connor up on that job offer, aren't you? That's the appointment you're going to after this. Don't lie to me, Daniel. I can tell when you're lying.'

'You don't have much faith in me, do you? In fact I'm going round to see Molloy. He offered me a chance to turn Connor in and I'm going to take it. That's the appointment I have – with Detective Molloy.'

She opened her mouth, closed it again.

'I loved you from the first moment I saw you at the Grande Ballroom, Evie, but you went for Billy. You thought he was the man for you, but he wasn't. I am. And I'm going to prove it to you if it takes me the rest of my life.'

She couldn't think of an answer.

His words echoed in her head, around and around like an aeroplane looping the loop, as she climbed out of the car and began to walk. When she looked back Daniel was still waiting. Watching over her as he always did.

Honourable.

Billy's voice spoke to her for the first time since he had died that dreadful day. *Daniel's a good man, Evie. Don't you let him go now . . .*

She was smiling when she opened the front door.

'Gwen?' she called.

A sound, the scrape of a shoe on the floor, the creak of a chair. She walked towards the kitchen, still thinking of Daniel and still smiling.

And froze.

Gwen was tied to the kitchen chair. There was a cloth around her mouth to stop her crying out. Her face was flushed and streaked with tears, her eyes bulging with the warning she couldn't give. The kitchen table was littered with the evidence of her interrupted meal preparation – a chicken and half done vegetables and her favourite bone handled peeler, spilling out from under an upturned baking tray.

Evie stepped forward, shocked, unable to utter a word. Her head swung one way and then the other, searching for Jimmy. She couldn't see him. 'Gwen!' she croaked at last. 'What's happened!' She ran to help her and as she did, Gwen looked beyond her and made an urgent throaty sound.

An arm came around from behind, snaking tight around her throat. Suddenly she couldn't breathe.

'Evie, you're late.' Leo's warm voice tickled her ear, his tone gently admonishing. 'We've been waiting for you.'

'Hide, hide, Evangeline. Do not move for your life.'

The cupboard was small and smelt of age and beeswax. And Genevieve, who a moment before had been laughing and brushing Evie's hair before the mistress's mirror, was suddenly very afraid.

'It will be all right, Evie. I will be back very soon to take you home.'

The gleaming red stone swung between her breasts and Evie reached out to touch it. But Genevieve caught her fingers and squeezed them.

'Quiet, you must be very very quiet . . . Not a peep from you, Evangeline. Do not move. Do not speak. Not until I come back for you.'

And then there was silence. Evie was uncomfortable in her hiding place, but she did not move. She did not often come to the big house and it frightened her. The people in it frightened her – the old man with his wicked eyes, the

*lady with the cold smile and the young men, one so fair
and one so dark. Genevieve said she was not supposed to
be here, and that there would be trouble if she was found.
But it was such a treat for her and where was the harm
. . .?*

The cupboard door was not quite closed. It had not
caught when Genevieve had shut it. She could see the
blue window. So beautiful, so blue. She tried to pick out
as many of the birds as she could and pretend that they
were alive with their wings flapping and their songs ring-
ing all about her.

And then suddenly there was a thump. Voices, growing louder and louder. Evie heard Genevieve cry out
and then a door slammed. Footsteps, running. Then, a
moment later, a man's footsteps, following. Uneven footsteps, one leg dragging a little after the other. She peeped
out and saw Leo reach the staircase and go down. Young
and handsome, fair haired. His eyes as blue as the window.

Evie stayed and waited, but nothing happened. The
light faded and darkness came and at last she crept out,
stiff and hurting, her tummy aching and her face cold and
wet with tears.

A servant found her on the stairs crying and carried her
down to her father.

'Mama?' she whispered, but no one knew where Genevieve was. No one could find her. There was a room, and
all the family from the house were there.

'Did she see you?' the woman kept saying to Leo, over
and over again. 'Did the child see you?' Then, to her
father, 'Will she speak of it?'

And her father, looking down on her. Her father, who
Mama whispered wasn't her real father at all, said, 'She
won't say anything, ma'am. I will see to it.'

❦

'Leo,' she croaked.

He had a gun. It looked like one he had kept since the war and he placed it against her breast.

'I'm sorry, Evie, but you brought this upon yourself. What were you hoping for, coming to Blue Waters and pretending to see Genevieve's ghost? Money? Was that it? I knew at Muriel's that you were up to something. *Au secours!*' He laughed. 'Very good. I couldn't resist persuading Leila to ask you to Blue Waters.'

'Leila knew.'

'Of course. Genevieve was a nuisance and someone had to do it. She was never going to be happy married off to old Frederick. You're like her, you know. Incurably romantic and far too trusting.'

'Leo – your father is dead. You don't have to protect him anymore. You –' Even as she said it, she knew. She knew.

'What has my father got to do with it? I killed Genevieve. I lured her down to the tunnel under the house and left her there. Never been opened up since. Dangerous, you see.'

'But Henry is my father! Isn't he?'

Leo laughed again. 'I think you'll find that's me. I was Genevieve's lover. She liked to play with fire and sometimes she got burnt. But she couldn't bring herself to stop.'

A flicker at the edge of her vision. For a brief moment it was Genevieve in her silver dress, her face solemn, her pale eyes accusing as they rested on Leo. And then Genevieve was gone and it was Daniel. The little gun was in his hand, but he couldn't use it without the bullet hitting Evie.

Leo must have seen him, too, or sensed him. He lifted his own gun and fired. Daniel went down, but it gave Evie the chance she needed. She reached out for Gwen's favourite bone handled peeling knife, hidden among the vegetables on the table, and drove it backwards, into the body behind her.

Leo cried out in agony, fell against the wall and slid down.

Without looking to see how badly hurt he was, Evie stumbled away and dropped down beside Daniel's body. There was a lot of blood. It spread over his white shirt and his face was paler than she had ever seen it. She whispered his name over and over as she kissed him.

I'm going to prove it to you, if it takes the rest of my life . . . 'I love you,' she said. 'Daniel, I love you.'

Behind her, Leo's breathing was growing more strained. She looked around and saw that Gwen was still tied up. She climbed to her feet and went to untie her, not knowing what else to do.

'Where's Jimmy?' she asked.

'Upstairs, asleep, bless him,' Gwen whispered as if her throat hurt. 'Go to Vi's, Evie. She has a telephone. Get her to call for the police and the doctor. Quick now!'

Evie ran out into Earle Street. The last thing she saw was Gwen, bending over Daniel and pressing her apron to his chest.

EPILOGUE

E ARLE STREET WAS JUST WAKING up. Vi Morgan had been over to say her goodbyes, as had several of their other neighbours. Everyone said they were sorry to see them go and that Earle Street just wouldn't be the same without them.

The gangly boy whom Evie'd thought was the latest member of the push had turned out to be employed by Leo Grieves to watch her. He had seen her coming and going and he had seen Diana's visit. Leo had worried about that – Diana knew enough to be dangerous and she was inclined to talk when she'd had too much to drink.

Evie and Gwen stood on the footpath, their suitcases beside them. Jimmy was safe in Evie's arms.

'Shouldn't be much longer,' she said, smiling as Gwen craned her neck up and down the street.

Leo had been taken into custody. Detective Molloy had led his men to Blue Waters and found Genevieve's body. She was still wearing the ruby, just as Evie had said and a silver evening dress wrapped her bones. Leila was certain her son would go free, but Raymond had made a statement before he'd taken Diana on a cruise to California, and rumour said they weren't coming back.

Evie had received an envelope, no note with it, but she knew it was from Frederick Woodward. Why had he sent it? She still wasn't sure. She liked to think it was an attempt at an apology, but more likely it was his revenge on the family he had protected for so long and who had abandoned him at the end.

The envelope had contained a birth certificate, dated 15th May 1904, for Evangeline Woodward, giving her parents' names as Frederick and Genevieve. As she took the certificate out of the envelope, two smaller pieces of paper had fallen to the floor. One was a document stating that Frederick and Genevieve had been legally joined in marriage on 20th December 1903 – five months before Evie was born. The other was Frederick's marriage to Amy Knowles, seamstress, in 1908.

Who better to hush up a scandal than a faithful family servant? Except that the affair had gone on after the marriage. Perhaps Genevieve couldn't give Leo up. Perhaps she had threatened him in some way and he had decided to kill her. But he hadn't known that Evie was there. Genevieve had hidden their daughter and led him away from her.

'We're going to our nice new house,' Gwen was tickling Jimmy under the chin and he giggled. 'Lucky Jimmy.'

'Lucky Gwen,' Evie said.

And Lucky Evie.

'There it is! At last!' Gwen fluttered about the cases as the car turned the corner. Evie watched it come, her smile growing. It drew up and the door opened and Daniel climbed out. He met her eyes over the bonnet.

He looked thinner than he should have been, and paler, but he was alive. It had been a near thing, but he had survived. He had saved her life, hers and Gwen's and Jimmy's, but nearly died himself. He had seen someone standing in the garden at number 5, Earle Street, he had said. Someone who shouldn't have been there.

'Who?' Evie had asked him, when he was well enough to talk.

But he'd only shaken his head. Evie had a feeling he would tell her one day, and she also had a feeling she knew who it was that he had seen.

Genevieve was still saving her life.

'Well, come on, Daniel, and help with the cases!' Gwen called, but she was smiling and her eyes sparkled.

Lots of things were about to change and all for the better.

Daniel winked at Evie and walked around the car to help, ruffling Jimmy's hair as he passed.

At that moment Evie's happiness bubbled over.

ABOUT THE AUTHOR

KAYE DOBBIE HAS BEEN WRITING professionally ever since she won the Big River short story contest at the age of eighteen. Her career has undergone many changes, including writing Australian historical fiction under the name Lilly Sommers, to romance written as Sara Bennett and published in the US and Australia. Her books have been translated into many languages. She is currently writing under her 'proper' name, Kaye Dobbie, and is published by Harlequin Mira in Australia and Weltbild in Germany. Kaye lives on the central Victorian goldfields with her husband and three very important cats.

www.kayedobbie.com
www.facebook.com/KayedobbieAuthor
Sign up to her Newsletter for the latest.

OTHER BOOKS BY THE AUTHOR

Colours of Gold
Sweet Wattle Creek
Mackenzie Crossing
Willow Tree Bend
and
When Shadows Fall